Darkwell Bled (author)
Darkwell Bled's The Soul Weaver
ISBN 978-0-6489191-2-4

1. FICTION / HORROR
2. FICTION / FANTASY

Typeset Athelas 10/14

Cover and In-book illustration by Laura Smith

DEDICATIONS

To my wonderful Grandad,
who would have probably preferred this
were a western.

And to my darling Mother,
who was vexed when the previous book
was not dedicated to her.

contents

Prologue

Prologue

Saturday, September 26th. 11:55pm.

George Atwell was drunk. He had been drinking since his shift had begun and now, having clocked off for the night, he fanged his car past the local high school, burped, and thanked the lord for how few police patrol the hills of Clarke Valley. When he was younger he had taken his work more seriously, but years of 'on the job' experience had taught him two things: that no one in Clarke Valley wants to break into a power station, and that a ten-hour evening shift goes much faster when you're on the sauce. By shift's end, he'd drunk all that he had brought with him that day.

He swerved, and he sped, and he was rarely in the correct lane.

In the night's darkness the narrow road and its markers were difficult to see, and while rounding a corner his beat-up Dodge listed into the dirt and scraped its rusted panelling along the guardrail that runs the length of Hansen Road. The warring metals screamed and George muttered to himself while dully wondering whether an outside observer might see sparks. His TV had been broken for over a year now, but he could well imagine how it might look.

Just like an action movie.

With a heave, he pulled the steering wheel to the left and the Dodge moved away from the lightly guarded heavy-drop. If another car had been coming from the opposite direction, then George would almost certainly have suffered a head-on collision, but with the time of night as it was he fancied his chances. Approaching the next corner, he started to steer with his knees, and fumbled a cigarette from his breast pocket. Pulling out the car's lighter, he held its hot tip to the cigarette's butt and was shocked to see a dark figure standing in the centre of the road.

He swore, the Dodge's tyres screeched – favoured the left – and spun.

After two dizzying rotations the car eventually came to a stop, facing uphill in the direction from which it had come, and George vomited. Woozy, worried, and covered in his own puke, he opened the rusty car door, stumbled several steps away from the vehicle and called out – then stopped, confused by his solitude.

The figure was gone and something felt... off.

There was a wrongness in the air and fear began to pin-prick cold sweat across his spine and skull. Taking two panicked steps backwards, George grappled clumsily with his belt. The clips that connected the various keys, whistle and torch to his person were slick with vomit and, while it only took seconds for him to free the torch from its bonds, time dragged. When finally the clip opened and George shone the bright beam towards where he had seen the figure, he gave out his best and most authoritative "Hey!"

... and still there was nothing.

No dark figure stood on Hansen Road and George was completely alone.

Skittishly he scanned the area with his small spot-light, stepping towards the blank point in the bitumen where he had seen the figure. He wondered if someone was playing a prank on him. He imagined some snot-nosed teenagers laughing their arses off as he stumbled shakily around in the dark. Or perhaps what he had seen hadn't been there at all and was merely a hallucination. Having never before experienced such an effect from his drinking, he dismissed this theory and instead set out to further examine the area, quickly discovering that there were two sets of skid-marks near where he had spun. The first – his own vehicle's – led toward his car, while the second set twisted heavily to the right. Like a dachshund tracking a scent, George drunkenly followed this foreign set of tyre marks and found that they ran off into the dirt and directly through a section of guardrail that had been completely destroyed.

"Shit," he muttered softly, looking down the cliff face at broken branches, shattered trees and impenetrable darkness.

Forgetting about the figure, George took two steps away from the cliff and considered whether the guardrail had been like this earlier. *Had there been a crash recently? Had he seen the guardrail broken on his way to work? Had it been like this for weeks? Months?* As the questions ran through his mind, he paced up and down the road, kneading his fists into his eyes and wishing that he were much more sober. On the one hand, George felt that he could not be certain he had seen this section of broken railing before tonight and if it were new, then someone could still be down there. On the other hand, regardless of how old or new the signs of the crash were, if he were to report them to the police he would almost certainly be breathalysed. He would be found to be driving under the influence. He would lose his job, his licence, and possibly even be blamed for the crash. As he worried, he slowly began to feel as though he were being watched.

Turning, he frantically darted his torchlight in search of the observer, trying and failing to convince himself that it was merely his imagined teenage pranksters – but still, he was alone. Frozen in fear and trembling, he let out a pathetic sob. George could not say how long he remained this way – glued to the middle of the road and shaking – but it was not until the shrill screech of a bird from somewhere unseen that he snapped out of it. In the lonely darkness the bird sound had seemed unnaturally loud. It caused him to jump, drop his torch, and run. He moved faster than his bung knee had carried him since high school football and within moments the old Dodge's tyres were squealing the car back towards town.

As he drove he whispered quiet assurances to himself. "That wasn't anything," he said, glancing at the rearview mirror. "There isn't anything there and if there was, then it was just some punk kids," he continued, losing sight of the empty patch of road while rounding the next turn.

For the rest of the journey and while lying in bed that night, George repeated these reassurances to himself ad nauseum. When morning finally came, he made his breakfast of scrambled eggs and tried to force himself to smile at the events of his drive home. He laughed at how cowardly it must have looked for a 47-year-old security guard – covered in his own vomit – to get the jitters from a drunken hallucination and to jump at a loud bird. He even found himself able to appreciate the possible pranksters and how expertly they had scared him, if they had.

Aside from attending work, George was largely a hermit. He did not socialise, he did not read, and with his TV out of commission his information of current events was limited. He had no way of knowing that the crash that had caused the broken guardrail on Hansen Road had been covered in the media and gossipped over for a full week leading up to his incident. If he had known, then he perhaps wouldn't have been able to brush off his night and the strange figure he'd seen so easily.

In blissful ignorance, he sipped his coffee and enjoyed his eggs.

Part 1: The Ghost

Analeigh Harris sat in the small funeral chapel and fought back tears. To her left along the hard wooden bench sat two of her oldest friends, Alice Crane and Davey Rains. To her right was an empty space habitually left open for a third close friend – the very person they had gathered to farewell. The room was full of mourners draped in black and at the end of the room, behind the funeral celebrant and her lectern, sat a dark casket that held the remains of Ryan Crosnor.

The casket was closed.

At only seventeen years of age, Analeigh had never before been to a funeral. Despite this, it had so far progressed much as she imagined most funerals would. The father of the deceased had said some nice words and the celebrant had led those attending in a psalm. Analeigh had gone along with this and had sung the words distributed to them on small pamphlets – though she knew for a fact Ryan had never been remotely religious. In life he had fluctuated somewhere between an agnostic and a slightly belligerent atheist, and had never willingly attended church since baptism. Ryan's parents, however, were religious and Analeigh supposed this was more for their sake than for his.

Despite Ryan's lack of faith, such religious overtones did not seem to Analeigh as bizarre or out of place. This was largely because until today her only experience with such ceremonies had come from movies, and she could

11

not recall having ever seen a funeral on TV that was not overtly religious. If anything, with those TV funerals often being held in giant marbled cathedrals with echoed chambers and golden crosses, Ryan's funeral within the small carpeted chapel that sat on cemetery grounds, was quieter and less dramatic than she had been led to expect. There was no organ angelically droning out lofty notes, but instead a recording playing tinnily through a speaker mounted in the corner of the room. The weather outside was not gloomy – stormy and overcast, but tinged orange by an early October Sun. The mourners were quiet and reserved – there were no aggrieved widows dramatically weeping over an open casket.

And Ryan's casket was closed.

Whether or not a funeral was to have an open casket was something Analeigh had discovered attendees were not informed of beforehand. She had been told the time and place, but nothing of the presentation of the body. Having seen open caskets as commonplace in film, she had spent much of the morning bracing herself for the possibility that she might see a corpse, and felt certain that she did not have it within herself to look upon death in such an unfiltered form. Knowing her friend was dead and seeing him dead were two entirely different affairs and when first entering the chapel Analeigh had been more than relieved to find the casket – *Ryan's casket* – closed. On reflection, it was only because it was closed that she felt she was able to stand being in the room.

A casket was clean, clinical, and strangely impersonal. There was nothing about the wooden box which sat before them that spoke to who or what Ryan had been. Even so, when looking at the dark box Analeigh couldn't help visualising Ryan's corpse lying within – dreadfully pale and looking as though it were simply sleeping. The mental image was horrible, yet she knew that it was entirely of her mind's own creation, and likely better than the truth. She knew that within the box he would not really be covered in make-up, wearing a placid expression, and looking as though he were resting serenely. She knew that, as terrible as the thought of her friend's imagined too-calm face was, the reality of his final appearance was likely much worse, and that even if Ryan's parents had wanted an open casket, the brutality of his death would almost certainly have made it an impossibility. The words 'drowned', 'broken', and 'battered' began to run through her mind, and she shuddered and let out a sob.

Analeigh had tried in vain to ignore the details of Ryan's grotesque death since the discovery of his vehicle at the base of Hansen Road two weeks prior, but it had been heavily reported in the paper, on the news, and parroted by schoolyard rumour. She could see every headline, and she could hear every bulletin, and each day as she drove to and from school she passed the curve from which his car had left the road and found it impossible not to imagine the fear he must have felt as it had tumbled over. With these thoughts, more words rushed into Analeigh's

13

mind like 'rolling', 'crashing', 'bending', 'bouncing', 'freezing', 'choking'... 'drowning' – until a squeeze of her hand brought her back to the present and forced her to relax. She shot a sideways glance to her left and then down at her hand, which was wrapped in Alice's. There was movement around them now, indicating that the funeral had concluded, while people in the pews in front began to stand. Row by row they each collected a flower, filed past the casket, and deposited it atop, before walking down the aisle and into a small room that connected the chapel for instant coffee and dry biscuits. Dropping a flower onto a wooden box did not seem like an adequate farewell to Analeigh but she could not imagine what would, so she dropped her flower and followed Alice and Davey down the aisle. As she walked, she did her best not to cast her eyes towards the side door, which was meant for the dead. From that door, the gravediggers would soon collect Ryan, carry him out to the cemetery – towards the dark hole they had dug him – and he would be gone, but she wasn't going to think about that.

Within the secondary room the three friends stood quietly. Once more an empty space had reflexively been left for Ryan – his absence made visible. Clarke Valley was a small town where almost everyone knew everyone. Analeigh had known Alice and Davey since diapers and Ryan soon after. Their parents had been friends since their own kindergarten days and had set up playdates between their children as a chance to catch up themselves. The vibe in the room was strange to Analeigh. With almost all of her classmates present – their families and friends – this crowd would have caused a rambunctious party had they been gathered for any other occasion. Instead, the large group spoke in overwhelmingly quiet whispers and as Analeigh shifted her attention away from them and back towards her friends, she wished that one would speak to break the tension.

Finally, Alice did. "It feels like a party where everyone's too afraid to dance," she whispered with the automatic quietness reserved for libraries and funerals.

"They're not playing my song," responded Davey with a dry levity that only his sad eyes betrayed as false.

Analeigh smiled at the exchange. Alice and Davey had always had an easy banter between them. Often it made her jealous, but today she found it extremely comforting. Before Alice could return a witticism of her own, the trio were joined by Ryan's father, who cut through the crowd towards them and stood in Ryan's empty open space.

"Thanks for coming, kids," he said softly.

"Of course," said Alice. "It was a beautiful ceremony."

Mr Crosnor placed a hand on her shoulder, nodded in solemn thanks, then turned and disappeared back into the crowd to mingle with other guests.

"*A beautiful ceremony*?" Davey repeated, genuinely unsure how a funeral could be viewed as anything but tragic.

Alice shrugged. "People kept saying it at my mum's wake... I think it's just something you say."

While they talked Analeigh watched Mr Crosnor cut through the crowd, eventually stopping to join a pudgy woman and her tall son in the corner of the room. The boy was wearing a nice suit – almost all the boys were. With school formal only two months away, many students had today worn the attire already purchased for that more joyful occasion. For a brief moment Analeigh found herself thinking about the suit Ryan had bought and would never wear. It probably hung in his closet right next to the costume he had ready for Halloween, now only four weeks away. Each year the four friends would go trick or treating with Alice's younger sister and then go to a house party at their friend Jackson's. The horror elements of Halloween had always been more up Alice's alley than Analeigh's, but she had to admit she enjoyed dressing up and always liked a good party. They had been making Halloween plans and brainstorming costume ideas the day before Ryan died, and Analeigh tried and failed not to think how Ryan had excitedly told them he already had his costume ready, or how he had planned to go as a zombie.

"I can't believe Cole is here," Davey muttered, snapping Analeigh's focus back onto the tall boy.

The boy was Cole Sheridan.

Analeigh *hated* Cole.

Cole was the local blowhard and school bully, and it was well known that he both picked on Davey, and had picked on Ryan, on a near-daily basis. While Davey usually took these insults on the chin, Ryan had always taken them to heart. Unlike Davey, Ryan could never simply walk away from Cole, always feeling as though he had something to prove yet rarely managing to do so. As Ryan was the smallest on a football team of unusually tall boys, it was no secret that Cole constantly mocked him throughout every game and training session they played. It was also no secret that training happened to be every Saturday night, or that on the night of Saturday the 19th of September – the night of Ryan's death – Cole had been especially vicious towards him. They had been training late and after one too many insults, purposefully misthrown passes, and unnecessarily brutal tackles, Ryan had left in a hurry, down the hill, and over the cliff.

The local news the next day had merely said that Ryan died when his car went over a ledge on his drive home from school. The police had blamed speed and inexperience – suggesting that he had likely been travelling 20 km/h over the speed limit at the time. His car had failed to make a tight turn, smashed through the railing, and gone over the steep edge of Hansen Road before rolling multiple times and eventually landing upside-down in the river that ran through the ravine. Despite the substantial injuries Ryan incurred during the crash, it was the river water that had eventually gotten him, with 'drowning' listed as his official cause of death. Around the schoolyard, some rumours suggested suicide, while others believed Ryan had just been too upset to pay proper attention to safety. Regardless – whatever the case may be – almost everyone agreed that were it not for Cole, Ryan would still be alive.

And now Cole was at Ryan's funeral.

"He has some damn nerve," said Davey, shaking his head in disbelief.

"It would've been worse if he hadn't come," answered Alice, trying – as always – to see the good in people.

"Would it?" asked Analeigh, unable to imagine any situation made worse by Cole's absence.

Alice frowned and considered the question, debating within herself whether she truly believed what she had said, or was simply being optimistic. Deciding that she wanted to believe it, if nothing else, she shrugged, and suggested that the situation might have made him turn over a new leaf.

Analeigh was not convinced. "A new leaf?" she repeated incredulously, matching Alice's frown with a scowl.

Realising that her attempted optimism had angered her friend, Alice gave no further response and an awkward silence fell over the trio. They each took a sip of their rapidly cooling coffees and Analeigh wished that she had been less standoffish. As they stood quietly, Mr Crosnor turned away from the Sheridans and walked back toward the centre of the room while Davey, not enjoying the silence, finished his coffee and reignited the conversation.

"Well, new leaves notwithstanding, I wouldn't want him here now if I were—".

"—This might not be the time," Alice cut in with an urgent whisper, fearing that Ryan's father was now within earshot and might become upset by their unpleasant conversation. Understanding, Davey nodded as Mr Crosnor cleared his throat.

"Thank you, everyone, for coming. We've got to clear out now. If you would like to come back to the Crosnor home, we are going to have a few quiet drinks. If you can't make it that's fine and thanks again for helping to farewell Ryan."

There were a few polite comments quietly spoken in encouragement, then the gathering slowly made their way outside. While Analeigh pulled her car out of the small town's cemetery, she couldn't help but reflect on her first funeral and how it had made her feel. There was a deep sadness within her, but no real sense of closure. Intellectually, she noted that she had perhaps simply not yet come to terms with Ryan's death. Despite this, regardless of how she rationalised it, she realised that she still could not believe Ryan was truly gone.

It was early October in Clarke Valley and, in stark contrast to the sombre nature of Saturday's funeral, Halloween's cartoony renditions of death had started to appear. Pumpkins were beginning to be carved and sat on porches, Beistle die-cuts brightly stuck to windows, and cotton balls strung thin between trees – made up to look like cobwebs. As the town was actively being transformed, so too were subconscious changes taking place, with everyday sights and sounds adopting new and ominous meanings. Black cats, dark shadows, and the forest-covered hills that surround the town were starting to be looked upon with good-natured superstition and fun-loving fear. Everything was coloured orange and black, and the magic of the spooky season was in the air – invading the subconscious and inspiring wonder. And Davey, Alice, and Analeigh had to go to school, and Melvin was dating a cheerleader.

Melvin was pasty, lanky, heavily asthmatic, and not a looker.

Helen – *the cheerleader* – was tall, and beautiful, and tanned, and fit. And she was dating Melvin.

Melvin was dating a cheerleader and that wasn't even the most unbelievable news being discussed by students aboard one of the aged yellow buses during the Monday morning commute. As the bus lurched and coughed its way up the hill, classmates giggled to one another and gave sideways glances towards Melvin and Helen, who

20

sat together near the back, but when passing the broken railing along Hansen Road the subject of their discussion quickly changed. Those on the left side of the vehicle pointed out the window and whispered harshly, while those on the right stood from their seats to get a better view. By the time the bus pulled into student parking and began to unload, no student aboard was unaware of the day's rumours.

For years Alice, Davey, and Analeigh had themselves been forced to rely on these buses as their way up the winding track of Hansen Road. This had changed only recently when each of them had finally gotten licences and cars of their own – a newfound freedom that had cost Ryan dearly. Had Alice been on the bus, she would have already known, and eagerly taken part in the development of the morning's whispers. Instead, she first learned of them as they spread. From the bus the rumours were passed from those who had just arrived to those now arriving, then beyond. While she sat awaiting her friends at their usual shaded wooden bench and table between the classroom buildings and oval, several small groups of gossipers walked past her, and she eavesdropped intently. As Alice listened she learned that, while the graduating class of Clarke Valley High *should* have been devoting their attention to upcoming exams, instead, much of what was being discussed was Melvin and Helen, magic potions, and *the ghost*. When finally joined by Davey, she excitedly informed him of what she had heard, and he snorted at the news.

"I think it's unbelievable," he answered, shaking his head in disbelief. His mind had learned to dismiss such fanciful things, and the idea of ghosts and magic potions was not something he was willing to accept.

Behind him Alice could see that Analeigh's car had pulled into student parking and that she was making her way towards them.

"I know! It's – well, it's incredible," Alice enthused.

"I said *unbelievable*, not incredible," corrected Davey. "As in I don't believe it," he clarified. "Especially not the part about Melvin and Helen," he added in jest.

"Well, I don't know!" smiled Alice, distracted by the mention of the more grounded rumour, "I think it's kind of cute!"

"Cute?" parroted Analeigh, sliding onto the bench beside Davey. She had caught a partial whiff of the day's rumours during the short walk from the parking lot and, having heard something about a ghost, now joined her friends mid-conversation, and in utter confusion. "I think it's more macabre than cute."

"Melvin and Helen are pretty mismatched, but *macabre* is maybe a little mean," laughed Davey, seeing that Analeigh had misread their current topic of discussion.

"Melvin and Helen?" Analeigh repeated in query.

"They're dating, or so I'm told,"

"But what's Melvin and Helen dating got to do with ghosts?" she asked.

"The two rumours are unrelated – I'm fairly certain," answered Davey.

"They're saying he used a love potion," whispered Alice.

"The ghost did?" asked Davey facetiously.

"No, Melvin did."

"And where would he have gotten that?"

"Maybe from the witch in the forest," suggested Alice, while Analeigh leaned in across the table to better hear the scandal.

"Oh, where else but from the forest witch?" said Davey shaking his head, unsurprised that Alice had so quickly tied this latest rumour to their town's most famous piece of folklore – the forest witch Mother Bombalan.

"You've *seen* her hut!" Alice reminded him, annoyed by how quickly he always dismissed such things.

Davey swallowed heavily at the memory. While to most people in Clarke Valley the witch was nothing more than a fun campfire story, the existence of a hut that local legend had always said was hers, was all too real. Venturing to the secluded structure was a rite of passage, and Davey – like most students – had once gone to it on a dare. Though years had passed since then, he could still easily recall the coils of fear that had tightened around him. How the unmarked path that led to the hut had seemed to lengthen before his eyes. How, despite his solitude, he had felt as though he were being watched. When Davey finally returned to the school oval and faced the older boys who had dared him in, he had tried to put on a brave face. He hadn't mentioned that he'd nearly choked on his own spit when spotting the strange structure and seeing that smoke was coming from its chimney. Since that day, he had long-grown out of his belief in witches, but even now he could not deny how scared and unsettled the old hut had made him feel.

"Yes," he finally agreed. "I've seen it."

"Therefore, hence, and thus – witches," Alice concluded with a laugh, having herself once ventured to the hut, seen nothing so ominous, and happily embraced the possibility of witches and their potions.

Analeigh did not laugh. It had been six years since the dare that sent her into the forest and, much like Davey, she could clearly recall seeing the creepy, gnarled-looking structure, and she shuddered at the memory of sighting a dark silhouette that had moved behind its grime-covered windows. She shook her head to clear her thoughts, while Davey did the same to clear his own.

"Witches, ghosts, and geeks dating cheerleaders," he listed. "I'm still not sure I believe any of this." He paused in reflection and then corrected himself. "Actually, no. I *am* sure that I *don't* believe any of this."

As he spoke, students filed past them towards the class-rooms in readiness for homegroup. Among them, Alice noted, were Melvin and Helen, who walked together hand in hand.

"Are you two an item now?" she called with a friendly smile.

"We are!" said Helen, beaming.

"Do you know anything about witchcraft?" mumbled Davey jokingly and received an angry glare for his troubles.

"What have you heard about the ghost?" Alice cut in, genuinely intrigued, and aiming to change the subject.

"You should ask Billy!" came the response.

"Where is he?"

"Not here today," answered Melvin,

"Rumour has it he's too freaked out," Helen added.

"Who started *this* rumour?

"His brother, James," whispered Helen confidentially to all those who would hear. "He says Billy wet the bed last night and woke up screaming."

"Because he saw a ghost?" Davey clarified, doubtfully raising an eyebrow.

"That's what James says."

"Did his brother say when and where he saw this supposed ghost?"

"Not when exactly – but night-time – the where was while heading home from school. He and a few friends had been drinking near the oval and James says Billy saw the ghost at a bend in the road."

25

"Along Hansen Road?" pressed Analeigh. Vaguely a nightmare that she had suffered came to her, but faded from her consciousness before she could think on it.

"Where the guardrail's broken," confirmed Helen, then paled at the implication of her statement and to whom she had said it.

The group went quiet and Analeigh flushed red. She didn't believe it for a second and the mere suggestion angered her.

"It sounds like he drank too much," Davey finally suggested, joining Analeigh in her annoyance and providing Helen with an out.

"Yes, probably!" agreed Melvin, who took Helen's hand and directed her away from the awkward situation. "We've got to get to homegroup," he said as they moved off.

"Yes," nodded Helen.

The couple left and the three friends stood in stunned silence until the bell rang, shaking them from their stupor and forcing them to head off towards their respective homegroups. Though that day the friends did not themselves engage in the discussion any further, they each heard continued talk of the ghost in every lesson they attended, and when Monday gave way to Tuesday, were disappointed to find that, rather than die down, the rumours had continued to grow, spread, and mutate.

Despite their best efforts, discussions were overheard and details learned. It was said that the ghost came out at midnight, and the claim that it showed up at the broken railing along Hansen Road was repeated with every telling. It was said that the ghost floated in the mist and that its eyes glowed red, and soon others (more people than was likely true) were claiming to have seen it themselves. One girl reported that her father, who worked at the power station, had spoken to someone who had seen the ghost as early as two weeks ago, while others claimed that the ghost only came out during the full Moon – though there had been no full Moon on the night Billy was reported to have seen it. While it perhaps should have been expected in light of the location of the sightings and how soon they had begun after the funeral, the wide-consensus on the supposed ghost's identity upset the friends more than anything else.

The ghost – people agreed – was that of Ryan Crosnor.

Wednesday, October 7th. 3:00am.

Analeigh slept in sweat and tears, and as she did, she dreamed.

In her dream it was midday and she walked the long coiled bitumen of Hansen Road while the Moon hung above like some obnoxiously ostentatious chandelier. It did not note as strange to Analeigh that the Moon was out during the day, and she instead accepted it with the unnoticed indifference commonly given to dream-time surrealism. The tread of the bitumen was thick and sticky, and she had to walk as though she were wading. Around her was silence. The trees that lined the road were all leafless branches which teemed with black ravens that watched her laboured trudge. Soon she came across an old man who stood in the middle of the road, sunk deep to his ankles. He asked for help and Analeigh offered her hand, but as the man grabbed for it the road swallowed him further. He sank to his knees and the beginnings of youth returned to his flesh, which then started to peel and bruise.

And the ravens cried and screamed.

The man sank to his waist and was no more than forty, and deep lesions were cut across his rapidly de-ageing skin.

The ravens beat their wings, causing winds like typhoons.

He sank to his chest and was a man in his mid-twenties, and his eyes had begun to bleed.

The ravens took flight, and blacked out the midday Moon.

He sank to his neck and the face that stared up at Analeigh was horribly deformed and terribly recognisable. The man who had de-aged had become a boy, and was now Ryan. As the sticky mud-like bitumen sludged its way into his throat, he gurgled a cry for help – and Analeigh awoke, soaked in sweat and fearing that she had wet the bed.

It was a dream that had become all too familiar. She had first experienced it the night following Ryan's funeral, but had been unable to recall details of it upon awakening. Since then she had experienced the nightmare three more times and, while it was only the last two that she could remember with perfect clarity, she felt certain that each had been identical.

Looking over at her bedside alarm clock with bleary eyes, she saw that it was 3am and regretted that (if the previous three nights were anything to go by) she would be unable to fall back asleep before the alarm blared its 7am wake-up. Sighing, she closed her eyes tightly and attempted to salvage some rest.

Wednesday, October 7th. 8:45am.

Massaging her head and trying to ignore the droning classroom chatter, Analeigh found herself wishing that she had stayed home sick in bed. She hadn't managed to fall back to sleep following her nightmare and instead had lain awake until sunrise, dwelling on the dream's strange imagery. Eating breakfast that morning, she had debated internally as to whether or not she should mention the dreams to Davey and Alice. Usually she would not hesitate to confide in her friends about such things, but she felt certain she knew exactly the conversation that would follow and already it exhausted her.

Alice – always the spiritualist – would read into the dreams too heavily and, before Analeigh would even have the chance to finish recounting them, she would be given several dozen different (and often contradictory) interpretations of their symbolism. Davey, on the other hand, would take the opposite yet equally exhausting approach, and attempt to downplay their importance entirely. He would claim that dreams were just our subconscious processing things. That the funeral and the schoolyard rumours had simply gotten her frazzled. It wouldn't matter that the dreams had started before she had heard the rumours – she had no doubt they would be blamed. It was perhaps the rumours themselves that were the main reason for her hesitation, as she feared that in discussing the dreams, the subject would quickly be bridged into that of the ghost – a conversation Analeigh had no interest partaking in, let alone starting. So far the friends had avoided discussing the unpleasant reminder of Ryan's death, and that was how she preferred it.

When lunch came, the trio sat at the bench and table and, while Alice and Davey talked, Analeigh chewed her sandwich in silence. She couldn't say what they were discussing – her thoughts were still too otherwise occupied. Sometimes a comment would be directed her way and she would give a noncommittal grunt or nod, then go on thinking – the dreams playing out in her mind and plaguing her thoughts. When she finished her sandwich, she absentmindedly glanced down at her watch and was shocked by the time. Lunch was almost over and she had done nothing but think. She hadn't fully realised just how preoccupied with the dreams she had become and regretted having wasted the chance to socialise with her friends. Second-guessing her decision to stay quiet on the matter, she opened her mouth to speak – unsure of what she intended to say even as she did so – but was immediately interrupted by a football which flew past her head and knocked over Davey's juice box, leaving it to pathetically gurgle its wasted contents into the grass.

"Heads up, Drizzle!" Cole yelled with deliberate lateness and walked over, followed by Steven and Jackson.

"Oh great, Cole's here." Analeigh groaned loud enough for the approaching boys to hear.

The remark caused Steven and Jackson to laugh, and Cole to bare his teeth in a smile that showed too much gum. Beyond the smile, he otherwise maintained his focus on Davey. "Hey, Drizzle, now that Melvin has a girl, you know you're officially the most frigid guy in school!" He spoke loudly despite standing a mere two metres away.

It was an insult that Davey had been expecting. Frankly, he was surprised it had taken Cole a full two days before he had weaponised Melvin's happiness against him. Such attacks were nothing new to Davey; Cole had been mocking his and Ryan's close, non-romantic friendship with Alice and Analeigh since they were eleven. Usually these attacks didn't faze him, but over the years they had caused Ryan a great deal of insecurity. Now, as Davey felt anger unexpectedly boil up, he realised it was because Cole was still playing the bully so soon after Ryan's funeral, rather than the insult itself, that had annoyed him. Gritting his teeth, he decided to sink to Cole's level and fight stupid with stupid. "I haven't seen you with too many women, Cole."

Unfazed by the rebuttal, Cole smiled mockingly. "Your problem isn't too many women, Drizzle, it's *two* many women," he said, holding up his fingers for emphasis. "At least when I'm with a girl, I'm actually dating her!" he added braggingly.

"That's purely theoretical, I assume?" Analeigh pitched in, unwilling to simply stand by and watch her friend be attacked.

Ignoring her comment, Cole continued to focus on Davey. He smiled cruelly and feigned genuine interest.

"What is it that you do at Alice's slumber parties, anyway? Just manicures, or pedicures too?"

The true answer to the question was 'watch bad movies and eat junk food' but, deciding to attack his ego, Analeigh instead winked, slipped one arm around Davey's elbow and with as much innuendo as she could muster, responded, "You have no idea what we get up to on our sleepovers."

Taking the hint and Davey's other arm, Alice added, "You couldn't even imagine!" just as suggestively.

"Good money says it's brushing Drizzle's hair and playing with dolls," answered Cole, though a deflated tone had invaded his voice.

"Now who's being frigid!" Analeigh chastised and stuck out her tongue.

Cole reddened, but from annoyance or embarrassment no one could tell. He looked as though he were going to say something more but the bell rang and, seemingly relieved by the excuse to leave, he instead mumbled something about having already received a late warning for class, then turned and walked away from the altercation. As he left, the other two boys who had been playing football with him did not follow.

"Oh yes, he's certainly turned over a new leaf," said Davey to Alice, good-naturedly mocking her hopeful suggestion from the funeral.

Alice frowned.

"I sometimes wish I could just sock him in the jaw," Analeigh remarked.

"Forget him," muttered Jackson. "He's just pissy I didn't invite him to my Halloween party this year."

"Why do you even hang out with him?!" Analeigh criticised in a tone that came out more accusatory than she had intended.

"He's on the team," replied Steven. He bounced the football once, thoughtfully, then in a downtrodden voice added, "And we don't have enough members left to get picky."

Feeling embarrassed, Analeigh blushed and looked away. In her grief over her fallen friend she had forgotten that others were missing him too. She attempted to apologise, but it caught in her throat and became a gurgle. Before she could try again, an annoyed teacher shouted from the classroom buildings something about tardiness and the passage of time, and the group was forced to disperse.

Thursday, October 8th. 8:20am.

When Analeigh arrived at school Thursday morning, she saw that a small but energetic crowd was gathered near the oval. Curious as to what the spectacle could be, she muscled her way in and discovered that Billy stood in the centre. This was the first time he had returned to school since the start of the rumours, and the gathered students were eagerly querying him about what they had heard and what he had seen. Among the growing crowd Billy looked small, pale and scared. At first he was unwilling to comment on the gossip, but when pressed he had confirmed it, admitting that he had seen a 'something' on Hansen Road. While Analeigh was grateful that Billy hadn't said it was **Ryan's ghost** he had seen, it hadn't really mattered. His confirmation of anything had been enough and now more people than ever were excitedly talking about the ghost, and whispering about Ryan.

With Alice, Davey, and Analeigh sharing no classes until the second half of the day, the friends were forced to bear the brunt of the rumours alone, and with the excitement of the supernatural involved, boundaries were crossed, and feelings not considered. In her last lesson before lunch, one especially callous individual asked Alice directly what her opinion on the ghost was, and whether she personally thought that the spirit was Ryan's. This had left her speechless. It wasn't that she hadn't considered it – she had. The supernatural was an obsession of hers, and the ghost's identity was practically all she had thought of since Helen had mentioned its location on Monday. But she had yet to talk to her friends about it, and felt that discussing the topic with anyone else beforehand would be a betrayal. Bringing up the topic had, however, proven difficult – any mention of the supposed ghost clearly upset Analeigh and annoyed Davey, and Alice did not like upsetting her friends. Despite this, it was something that Alice knew they would eventually need to discuss. While class continued around her, the question of the ghost's authenticity and identity played on her mind and slowly she started to work up the courage needed to address the topic with Analeigh and Davey herself. When class let up, the trio met at their usual shaded table, a glance was shared between them, and Alice felt a lump begin to form in her throat. Clearing it with a phlegmy cough, she bit the bullet, and attempted to start the conversation.

"You don't think—" she began.

"No," said Davey, cutting her off before she could get her thought out.

"It *is* the same spot where he crashed," she ventured hesitantly.

"Which is why stupid people started the rumour," spat Analeigh and immediately regretted her harshness. Her nightmares had continued and she had decided not to mention them to her friends. Each night it was the same thing – the ravens, the Moon and Ryan sinking into the road – and the dreams combined with the constant rumours at school, had given her little chance to relax. Taking a deep breath, she tried her best. "Sorry, Alice, I've... not been sleeping well," she admitted without elaboration. "Can we just change the subject?"

Alice forced a smile. "Of course, Ani."

And the trio passed the rest of the day by pointedly ignoring what all three were thinking, until the next morning when the early edition of the local paper was delivered and the subject of the ghost became unavoidable as a front-page headline.

Clarke Valley Gazette. Friday, October 9th.

'A Ghastly Ghostly Sighting!'

A young couple got more than they bargained for Wednesday night when their evening at the Hansen Road lookout (commonly known as 'Makeout Point') ended in horror, rather than romance. The couple, who have asked not to be named, claim that while returning down the hill at around midnight, they sighted a pale and ghost-like figure in the middle of the road. Swerving to avoid the ghastly ghoul, their car connected with the rockface and had to be towed. The spectre, they say, was then nowhere to be seen.

When asked, the young woman told this reporter that it was "the scariest thing [she] had ever seen", while the young man claims he was more scared of missing curfew. Neither were injured by the encounter and police have confirmed that the driver tested negative for drugs and alcohol; however, they suggest that pranksters, not poltergeists, are likely responsible for the sighting.

Speaking to the *Gazette*, Police Chief Braxton had this to say. "We have had several reports of similar sightings along Hansen Road and find it no coincidence that they occurred so near the school. We remind any would-be pranksters that Hansen Road is dark and dangerous, and would like to caution teenagers away from playing on the road and distracting drivers. No one was injured Wednesday night, but had the driver not swerved the prankster could have been killed, and had the driver swerved in the other direction, the couple could have been killed."

Chief Braxton's strong warning comes in the midst of an especially deadly year along Hansen Road, with multiple crashes and three deaths – one as recent as last month. The police are asking for anyone with knowledge of these pranks to visit the station on George Street or to call them anonymously on the non-emergency number listed below.

Friday, October 9th. 8:20am.

Analeigh slammed the newspaper down onto the wooden bench and swore. She had already read the article several times over – both the copy delivered to her home at breakfast and now the copy Alice had brought to school. Having been reported in the local paper, the ghost of Hansen Road was quickly developing a credibility it would have never received as schoolyard rumour alone, and was fast becoming a household topic. Across Clarke Valley no person gathered around a watercooler, patronising a coffee shop, or sitting in a hairdresser was not discussing the ghost, and any possibility of the friends avoiding the subject had entirely eroded. The reality of the ghost had become for many in the school an indisputable fact, and those who believed now cited the news article as proof. There were however, those (Davey amongst them) who remained unconvinced. He knew that countless publications had fancifully reported aliens, Big Foots, and even ghosts before, and felt that this morning's newspaper provided no more compelling evidence than the schoolyard rumours had.

"Just because it's in the paper does not make it true," he laid out to his friends before class.

"It's true enough that the journalist believes it," answered Alice.

Analeigh grunted.

"It does not, anywhere in that article, say the journalist *believes* it," objected Davey, aggressively pointing towards the paper for emphasis.

"It doesn't say he doesn't," countered Alice and Davey groaned.

Analeigh glanced down at the paper, re-read the comments made by Chief Braxton and frowned in annoyance. Until now she had assumed that Billy had simply gotten spooked after seeing some animal in the darkness and that everyone else had then gone on to scare themselves with stories. She had not considered the possibility that someone was pulling a practical joke. "If this is a prank, then whoever is doing it is trash," she declared.

"Yes," agreed Davey.

"If it is a prank," added Alice, unwilling to give up on the supernatural.

"If it is, then someone is purposefully taking advantage of Ryan's death," said Analeigh, realising that the decision to pull such a prank at the broken railing where he had died could not be a coincidence.

Davey and Alice fell silent.

In reaction to the newspaper article, homegroup was cancelled and an emergency whole-school assembly called. The principal was fuming – he had seen the morning paper and had spat his coffee across the dining room table at the police's insinuation his students were to blame. He considered the entire affair an embarrassment to the school and a personal insult. "If one of you little monsters is responsible," he growled, "then those who are will be caught."

The school hall had been deathly quiet, with students afraid that merely breathing would draw the principal's attention and suspicion. Not having fully planned what he would say, he had gone on to rave for over an hour, often going off on strange and unrelated tangents. But what came of the morning assembly was clear: the school was taking the apparent prank extremely seriously, they were working with the police, and they intended to suspend those responsible when caught. Further, if those responsible turned out to be from the graduating class, they would be barred from the graduation ceremonies.

By the time the assembly finally ended, it was 11:40am and the first several lessons of the day as well as recess had been missed. The principal had declared that he didn't want to hear people even talking about the ghost, but this had merely decreased the volume of conversation, rather than muting it. Because of their lack of shared classes, it wasn't until lunchtime that Analeigh, Alice, and Davey were able to get back together and continue their discussion.

"Do you really think it's just someone pulling a practical joke?" asked Alice dubiously, though knowing what Davey's answer would be.

"Yes," he predictably responded.

"But who?" Analeigh pondered aloud, more to herself than to her friends.

"Yeah," Alice nodded furiously. "If it is a prank, then how come no one is claiming it?"

Davey considered this and frowned. It *was* odd that no one was claiming responsibility for the hoax and that, despite all the rumours going around the school, none were speculating on who might be behind the alleged pranks. While this might simply have been because few students agreed with the police's assessment that the ghost was a mere hoax, it also meant that no one was quietly bragging about their involvement – if they had been, then it would have spread. Every practical joker likes to be the centre of attention, and the fact that those responsible were yet to have stepped forward into the limelight did seem strange to Davey, and the more that he thought about it, the more he realised that he had no idea why no one was claiming the prank. Alice – perfectly aware of this – patiently awaited his response.

"Because..." he finally said, gruffly clearing his throat, "because they don't want to get caught," he lamely finished, unable to convince even himself.

"Hmm," said Alice, unsatisfied.

"And that's only if anyone actually saw anything! It could be that there haven't even been any ghost sightings and people are just lying to seem important," he tried, feeling that this was a more convincing argument.

"I've never known Billy to be a liar," Analeigh stated distantly, still more focused on her internal thoughts than the ongoing discussion.

Davey turned to her with an exasperated expression while Alice beamed, pleased that Analeigh had somewhat sided with her. Smacking his lips together, he tried to formulate a response and then relented. "No," he agreed, "I've never known Billy to be a liar, either."

"So you believe in the ghost, then?" asked Alice – all but cheering.

"No, I guess I believe in the prankster," he allowed.

"Which brings us back to who," muttered Analeigh, taking the discussion full circle.

"Well, I have a theory about that," answered Davey, who had no real theory and was simply hoping to save face by successfully formulating one on the fly.

Alice – believing that a ghost was still more likely than a mysteriously coy prankster – was about to press him on his theory, but the bell rang and lunch came to an end. Not wanting to dawdle and give an already annoyed school faculty any excuse to punish them, the friends immediately started to gather their bags and head to class.

"I'll explain it tonight," he promised as they walked off in their different directions, feeling certain he could think of some logical explanation before they all met at Alice's for their weekly sleepover.

Once seated in the stale air of their respective classrooms, their lessons instantly dragged. Afternoons always felt longer on a Friday and within minutes of their teachers beginning to drone on about maths, art, and science, they each wished for their classes to hurry up and finish so that their night of pizza, terrible movies, and relaxation could begin.

Friday, October 9th. 3:40pm.

The school day eventually ended (as they are known to do) and the three friends headed back down the hill to Alice's home for their traditional weekly sleepover. As part of the lead-up to Halloween, the local TV station was playing a B-movie marathon each Friday night of October, but as that wouldn't start until II:00pm, the friends lazed about eating junk food, listening to music, and talking. Alice lay next to Analeigh on the floor of her small bedroom, while Davey slumped across a beanbag in the corner and a record spun twelve-bar blues. It was only the third sleepover since Ryan's death and his absence still felt strange and out of place. Despite being physically gone from their presence, he was not far from their minds, as the conversation almost immediately turned back to the ghost.

Each of them had, since lunchtime, grown stronger in their convictions. Alice now fully believed that something was wandering the hills of Clarke Valley – though was not convinced that it was necessarily Ryan rather than any number of possible spirits, nymphs, or forest deities. Davey had taken the polar opposite position and wasn't certain of anything beyond that it was absolutely not something supernatural, while Analeigh felt strongly that pranksters were responsible and wanted to find out who was making a mockery of her friend's death.

"You said you had a theory about who is doing it?" she prompted, turning her head to Davey.

He – having failed to come up with anything he was proud of – chewed his chips, downed a soft drink and avoided the question, until Analeigh prompted him again. "Pricks are who and the reason is because they're pricks." he offered.

"So more of a character profile than a specific person," mocked Alice and had a chip thrown at her for her trouble.

"Probably Cole?" Davey tried.

The record came to an end and Analeigh stood to flip it, then, thinking better of it, instead searched through Alice's collection to select a separate album. "I'm not sure Cole is smart enough for that, or subtle enough, or creative enough," she mused as she placed the needle down carefully. The music resumed and she slowly paced the room.

"Plus he's a terrible liar. Remember that one time we played cards at Jackson's?" Alice pointed out.

Davey found he couldn't argue against either of their points. "Okay..." he answered, drawn-out and reluctantly. "So not Cole, but I still say someone is pulling a prank."

"But who else would do it?" asked Alice.

He had no good answer. Quietly, he felt that it wasn't only Cole who lacked the skills necessary to pull off a hoax so successfully and instead believed these shortcomings extended to any of his fellow classmates who might be deranged enough to try. Despite this, he still found the idea that one (or several) of them had overcome such shortcomings astronomically more likely than the idea that ghosts exist. "I don't know who," he finally admitted. "But I still say it is an unknown someone causing these sightings, not an unknown something."

Analeigh stopped pacing and turned back to her friends with determination. "Well, why don't we just find out who that someone is?" she said with a smile and began to lay out her intentions.

Friday, October 9th. 11:45pm.

From the moment that they formulated their plan until 11:45pm, the sleepover progressed normally. They chatted and listened to music until the start of the movie marathon, and then watched as the schlocky late-night horror host introduced the first film, *Teenagers from Outer Space*. The movie played and they laughed, joked, and drank too much soft drink, and at times it felt almost like the old days before the accident. Analeigh had quietly worried about watching horror movies again. Even before Ryan's crash she had sometimes found scary movies hard to watch, and had grown concerned that recent real-life horrors might have further tainted her enjoyment of fictional ones. Fortunately, the film was so cheesy that this issue did not arise and, though they only saw partway through the film, they spent most of that time laughing, not screaming. Then, before the movie had concluded, Alice's bedside alarm clock went off – loudly announcing that it was time to leave.

The alarm rang just as a raygun reduced someone to a clean white prop skeleton and they began to sneak their way downstairs. A step creaked and the door to the room next to Alice's swung open. Standing in its doorway was Alice's six-year-old sister, Claire. She sensed adventure, wanted to come with them, and glared down with wide accusatory eyes. Knowing just how much trouble she would be in if caught out past dark, let alone if she took her sister with her, Alice insisted that her joining them

49

was absolutely not an option. Claire eventually relented, and instead settled for bribery – her silence bought with a tube of Alice's lipstick and a block of chocolate. Leaving her sitting on Alice's bed with their leftovers and the TV running, they went downstairs and opened the front door, feeling confident that the movie would fail to disturb even her. The air outside was beginning to cool and a light fog was forming in the valley which, in contrast to the film, was creating an eerie atmosphere. As they left the house they jumped at a cheap plastic ghost that hung on Alice's porch, realised they were on edge, and forced themselves to laugh at how they had been scared by such a comical-looking decoration. Leading the way, Alice and Davey walked down the porch steps towards Davey's car, and Analeigh, taking a deep breath to summon courage, followed.

The road on which Ryan had crashed was only a short distance from Alice's house – few places in the small town weren't – and they knew its twists and turns like the backs of their hands. By night, however, it was far less travelled, and as Davey wound the car through the darkness and its increasingly thick fog, his nervousness grew. The road was made up of narrow twists and blind corners, and lit only by a few scattered streetlights. There was a reason the road had the reputation of being dangerous at night, but he had never imagined just how dark and scary it became as midnight approached.

During their drive up the hill they only passed one other car – a battered Dodge that tore past them at a tremendous speed and belonged to a George Atwell. Unbeknown to them he had been the first to witness the supposed ghost of Hansen Road, and having since learned of the crash and made the connection, he now made sure to be long clear of the broken railing before midnight. Aside from Mr Atwell and the heavy, low-hanging fog, the road was clear. At 11:55pm Davey chucked an illegal U-turn and pulled his car close to the kerb opposite the broken barricade and the site of Ryan's death. The car's headlights cut through the fog and illuminated the twisted metal and absent chunk of roadside railing, revealing a few now-tattered floral wreaths and black skidmarks. Analeigh stared at the scene before her, finding it hard not to think how beyond the missing portion of fence was a long, rocky drop that led towards an unforgivingly strong river and cold death. Shivering as though she herself were in those waters, she leaned over from the passenger side seat and switched off Davey's headlights, leaving only moonlight to illuminate their surroundings.

"Maybe we shouldn't be here," whispered Alice. She had always been a fan of the idea of ghosts but, as she stared at the flowers and wreaths that had been placed in memory of her dead friend, decided it was an idea that she didn't necessarily want to see become a reality.

"At the very least, we should have brought the snacks," grumbled Davey, who couldn't help but wonder if Claire

– left unguarded with the pizza – would leave any slices for their return.

"Maybe we should just go home?" suggested Alice.

"I want to see what's happening and who is responsible," answered Analeigh with fixed determination.

Davey sighed. He considered the likelihood that the pranksters would strike tonight while they were there to be minimal. Even so, they had made the trip and he was not eager to have wasted the journey. "We might as well stay, it's only a few minutes 'til midnight and that's when they say the sightings were, right?"

"Uhh..." Alice's voice sounded uncertainly from the backseat.

"Right?" he pushed.

"Well, yes, but I think that came from the rumours... Billy never actually gave a specific time and even the newspaper only said *around* midnight," she responded.

Davey let out a long explosion of annoyed air through his nostrils as he dramatically slid down in his seat. "You mean to say—" he started, and was immediately hushed by Analeigh.

"Look." she whispered, suddenly seized by a strange, yet vaguely familiar feeling of fear, and all three squinted in the direction Analeigh pointed. Towards the guardrail and its missing section.

"I don't..." began Davey, squinting through the fog.

Alice was the second to see it. "On the ground," she whispered. "Where the road falls off."

"I – I – I," said Davey, his mouth falling agape.

When Analeigh had spotted it, it had merely been a hand – torn skin, broken bone, and ash-grey. By the time Davey spotted it, it was an arm, and then a head, and then a second arm. Dragging its way up and over the cliff edge from down which Ryan's car had plunged, it clawed as the Moon was eclipsed by clouds, and the creature was strange darkness.

Briefly Analeigh remembered the plot of a movie they had once watched at one of Alice's sleepovers, *The Old Dark House*, and reflexively she glanced around for strings and pulleys, but saw nothing to suggest trickery was afoot. The creature crawled with unnatural movements forced by disjointed limb and broken bone to the centre of the road, where slowly it rose, snapping bones, limbs, and ligaments into conformity until it stood jaggedly as the broken facsimile of a teenage boy, its face obscured by fog. With glacial speed its feet dragged forward as the Moon reclaimed its mantle and blue light cut through darkness to fall upon a young face of torment. Its cheek was shorn off to one side revealing bone and jaw where skin should have sat. Exposed rib showed through a shredded shirt and varsity jacket.

It was translucent, deformed, and dismembered.

In the moonlight only brown eyes – bright and undeniable – stood in testament to the creature's former identity, allowing the trio horrified recognition.

"Ryan." whispered Analeigh in awe and terror, her nightmare having become a reality.

The spirit moaned in agony as Davey swore and fumbled his car keys, desperately attempting to trigger the vehicle's ignition.

The ghost of Ryan had now crossed beyond the halfway point on the road and with its closed proximity further details of grizzly decomposition came into view. As it walked, it moaned as if in excruciating agony and confusion, then – at 55 km/h – a speeding car drove directly through the figure, before squealing to a halt.

And Ryan was gone.

"Its cheek was shorn off to one side revealing bone and jaw where skin should have sat. Exposed rib showed through a shredded shirt and varsity jacket."

Part 2: The Book

Saturday, October 10th. 12:10am.

After seconds that dragged like minutes, Davey succeeded in getting his keys into the ignition and peeled the car away at high speeds. Vaguely he worried that the driver of the other vehicle would recognise his and suspect them of being the pranksters, but mostly he was just scared. Within less time than the speed limit should have permitted, he was turning his car back into Alice's street and pulling it alongside the kerb out front her house.

For most of Davey's life he had been a sceptic – comfortably putting his stock in logic and science, and disregarding anything involving spiritualism, religion, and magic. It wasn't that he thought such things were entirely impossible, just that they were dramatically improbable. He had always claimed to have an open mind and identified himself as an agnostic – not an atheist. He could even recall having once told Alice that if there were proof of a god, then he'd be more likely to believe in one. Despite this, Davey had never actually expected to be faced with such proofs, and the reality of the situation shook him to the core.

There were parts of him that wanted to discredit what he had seen, blame the fog, the moonlight, or his own fatigue. *It was midnight and you went there expecting to see a ghost. Visibility was poor and you were tired. This is just confirmation bias combined with a bad case of the pareidolia effect!* a part of him cooed reassuringly in the back of his mind. But like a church minister who preaches chastity until caught partaking in some bizarre sexual deviancy, that voice had lost all credibility. There was no getting around it and there was no self-sophistry that could talk him out of it – the face had been Ryan's and so the ghost had been real.

Perhaps of the three of them the sighting had affected Davey the most, but each had been moved by the experience. Alice had gotten off the lightest – her belief in ghosts simply confirmed and her worldview left intact – but still she had found the experience somewhat terrifying. Analeigh was similarly scared, but her fear was overshadowed by sorrow; she alone of the trio was thinking not what this meant for themselves, but what this meant for Ryan. She had gone to the road expecting that the ghost would be proven false and hoping to catch the persons responsible for using Ryan's tragedy for their own morbid amusement. She left having learned that ghosts were real, that they suffered, and that Ryan was now one of them.

It was this apparent suffering that tormented Analeigh. Ryan had seemed as though he was in extreme pain – total agony – and while only minutes earlier she hadn't even fully believed in spirits, now her mind raced to think of what should, or could, be done to help one. She found herself wondering if they had seen Ryan's ghost by chance, or if this were truly a nightly ritual, and the possibility of the latter made her feel sick to the stomach. She wondered whether Ryan was even aware that he was dead, or if he was trying each night to crawl to safety, forever fuelled by the false belief that he could still be saved, and she shuddered at the horror he must experience while caught in this bizarre death loop. The sound of Ryan's painful moans continued to play noisily in the back of her mind as they quietly exited Davey's car, let themselves back into the house, creeped upstairs, and made their way back into Alice's room.

Claire had not saved them any pizza and, covered in grease, she was awoken by the soft thud of the bedroom door. Immediately, Alice and Davey began attempting to take their minds off of what they had just witnessed and – feeling nothing could be done tonight – Analeigh joined them. The movie had ended and another was already playing, which Alice switched off while a large gila monster chased down a group of rockabillies. To Claire's delight, the trio were more than willing to read her stories until she fell back asleep.

They welcomed the pastel colours, the simple plots, and the happy endings.

Little did Claire know that the friends continued to read through her stories long after she had dozed off, not ceasing until the morning Sun had begun to rise, and they had already worked through her full picture-book collection several times over.

Saturday, October 10th. 1:20pm.

With sunlight basking the small town of Clarke Valley, the three friends ignored their day's obligations and chose to remain at Alice's long into the afternoon. Davey, who should have been working at his father's hardware store, called in sick, while Alice and Analeigh, rather than studying for their finals, decided their minds were too otherwise occupied. They sat in the sunny warmth of Alice's backyard in complete silence. Few words had been said over breakfast or since, while each of them continued to privately process the events of the night in their own various ways.

Alice was lounging on a lawn chair with a large pile of books beside her. Had she been standing, the pile would have reached her waist. Her fascination with magic and mysticism dated back over a decade and some of the books in her collection had been with her since she was six – yet she now looked upon them with renewed interest. Several where talk of ghosts was quickly followed by accounts of unicorns and accompanied by brightly coloured illustrations she discarded as too fanciful, while others she marked with sticky notes that she should have been using in preparation for her upcoming biology exam. Among those Alice noted as relevant were excerpts from **Book XI** of the *Odyssey*, newspaper eyewitness accounts taken from all over the globe and recorded in a compendium, and collections of stories that focused on famous haunted locations spanning the Tower of London to forests in Japan. Included in the pile sat the latest addition to her collection – a copy of last Friday's local *Gazette*. Rather than hoping to find any specific information in her books, Alice read with the hope of gaining a wider understanding of ghosts in general.

Davey was undergoing a similar journey, but with a more focused goal in mind. With pen and paper in hand, he was desperately attempting to salvage his worldview. While there were plenty of topics (such as physics) that he had never fully understood, he had always been satisfied that there was a sound and scientific logic behind them and felt sure that with enough time and study he could fathom them. All things in this reality were, he believed, predictable, calculable, and therefore *knowable*. This belief had satisfactorily guided him for most of his life and, rather than entirely discard science, maths, and logic for ghosts, he intended to find a way in which spirits could be worked into his current understanding of the world. Ghosts, therefore – or whatever it was that he had seen last night – Davely had decided must be similarly knowable. They could not be supernatural in the true sense of the word, but must be something scientifically tangible and physical, and merely yet to have received the proper study necessary to understand them. They were, he theorised, no more actually supernatural than lightning had been to a caveman and, like electricity was eventually understood by man, so too did Davey hold out hope for an eventual understanding of the phenomenon he had witnessed.

He had written down and underlined the words: *All things in this world must be physical* and was now sucking on the end of his pen in contemplation. The apparition they witnessed had looked like Ryan, but was semi-transparent. This transparency alone was no real hurdle for Davey's entirely physical worldview. After all, wind, water, mist, and glass are all physical things that are either semi-transparent or entirely invisible. But the ghost had moved, and it had walked, and it had *looked* like Ryan. This was something that Davey was having more trouble getting his mind around. He jotted down a theory that what he had seen might have been some sort of residual "vapour" of Ryan – some essence that had been stored within Ryan's body and become moulded to its shape – then frowned, entirely unsatisfied by the idea. Perhaps this theory would have been more palpable if the spirit had not moved with apparent agency of its own. The ghost had not simply been static. It had climbed, and it had crawled, and it had stood, and it had walked – and those were all the sorts of things that indicate there had been some form of a mind at work, and Davey was not sure a mind could exist without a brain. He tapped his pen on the paper, underlined his mantra once more, and then, drawing a line from it, wrote down the extrapolation: *There can be no mind without a brain.*

Pausing to consider this new addition, he closed his eyes and reimagined the horrible image of his friend's ghost dragging itself across the road. He remembered having sighted torn ligaments and broken bones. These semi-transparent ghostly ligaments were conceivably responsible for the movements of Ryan's semi-transparent ghostly limbs. It was, Davey figured, further conceivable that if these ghost ligaments were causing the movement of ghost limbs, then perhaps within its ghost head there was a ghost brain. Perhaps Ryan's entire body (inner workings and all) had been somehow transmuted into this new state of unknown spirit energy. Or maybe no transformation had taken place after all, and what they had seen was not really Ryan but instead some kind of lesser copy – like a copper replica forged from a clay mould of a golden statue. Regardless of whether it was a copy or a transformation, Davey saw no reason that the unknown material that made up the Ryan-Image could not be entirely physical. Taking the pen from his mouth, he wrote down *spirit energy?* as a possible avenue of investigation, then did something he had never expected he would, and consulted Alice on ghosts. "Is there... is there anything in those books about ghost energy?" he asked uncomfortably.

"Loads!" came her surprised and energetic reply.

Questioning no further, he let out a slight "hmm" and went back to his theorising, only taking a brief moment to cast a concerned look towards Analeigh.

Analeigh was not reading and Analeigh was not writing. She was simply sitting and staring blankly, deep in thought. Despite her eyes being wide open, the events of the night past played back perfectly in her mind. Ryan's twisted, broken body. His deformed face. The look of pain and sorrow in his eyes. She, unlike Alice, had not spent her spare time studying ghosts and she, unlike Davey, had no great concerns about what the existence of spirits meant to the world scientifically, theologically, or otherwise. All that Analeigh found herself concerned with was that Ryan somehow, and in some form, still existed.

And he was suffering.

"We have to do something," she stated quietly, finally breaking her silence.

Alice and Davey both stopped and looked up from their respective tasks.

"Yeah, like never drive on Hansen Road at night again," replied Davey with forced flippancy.

"We have to do something *for Ryan*," Analeigh reiterated.

"Ryan's dead, Ani," he responded softly.

"*Undead*," corrected Alice, unsure if she was being helpful.

In truth, Davey was not certain how definitive any statement on Ryan's death could really be. If what they had seen was Ryan transmuted, then it was Ryan himself, but if it was merely energy moulded into his shape, then it was perhaps just some kind of echo. Davey was not sure how to answer the philosophical question of whether or not an echo of Ryan could be considered as actually Ryan and was unsure of exactly what could be done, regardless.

"Can you imagine what it must be like, to crawl and walk in the site of your death, broken and in pain, every goddamn night?" Analeigh pressed.

"I'm trying really hard not to," answered Davey faintly.

"He's our friend, so try."

Silence fell and Davey looked mildly guilty. Regardless of whether or not what they had seen was really Ryan, he didn't like the idea of his friend suffering in any form – echo or otherwise. "Well... what *can* we do about it?" he finally asked.

"We could go to the church?" suggested Alice, pulling a book from the middle of her pile and causing those above to topple. "Exorcisms are in here somewhere," she mumbled as she flicked through the pages.

"I don't think churches deal with that sort of thing anymore and besides, I'm not even sure Father Jones is even that religious," replied Davey.

"And I think exorcisms just banish ghosts, not... fix them?" recalled Analeigh, thinking back to some particularly scary films they had once watched. "We want to help Ryan, not just drive him away."

"So if we don't go to a spiritual expert, then we go to a magical one," suggested Alice.

"No," responded Davey, who guessed where this was heading and didn't like it.

"She's more likely to know about this than anyone else in town," Alice continued to push.

"Who?—*The witch*?!" gasped Analeigh in sudden understanding, then shuddered with unnerving fear.

"Sure, we know where she is and that she does magic," nodded Alice.

"*No*." repeated Davey, this time more forcefully.

"Well, why not?" asked Alice.

"Witches aren't real. If we go and try to find her, we will either: a) find the hut empty, b) find it full of squatters, or c) find a woman claiming to be a witch who will turn out to be nothing more than a scam artist selling snake oil," Davey listed off on his fingers matter of factly.

"Yesterday morning you would have said – or rather, did say – that ghosts aren't real."

Davey mumbled something incoherent under his breath. In truth, he now found that he was entirely uncertain as to whether or not he believed in the existence of witches. If he had taken the time to think about it, he would have realised that he was more annoyed at the loss of his once-strong convictions than he was at the prospect of searching out a local urban legend.

"So it's agreed?" asked Alice hesitantly.

"Whatever," he answered with a sigh. "But I'd still put good money on her being just some old hag who tries to scam us – if she even exists," he grumbled, digging his keys from his pocket while Analeigh let out a sigh of her own and Alice couldn't help but smile at the prospect of fulfilling a girlhood dream of meeting a real-life magic user.

Saturday, October 10th. 2:45pm.

In the warm mid-afternoon sun it was hard to believe that the road on which the trio now travelled was the same site as last night's gothic horrors. During the day, Hansen Road betrayed no signs of its nocturnal supernatural predilections and were it not for the broken railing and dark skidmarks, Analeigh could have well believed that it was a different road altogether.

Leaving the car in student parking at the top of the hill, Davey, Alice, and Analeigh made their way across the school oval and towards the forest. In just under three hours the football team would gather for practice, but until then the area was mostly empty save for Helen and Melvin, who gave them a disinterested wave from their picnic out on the grass. Despite the brightness of the Sun, the trees looked dark and as the friends crossed into the forest, they felt that it was instantly cooler. Though they knew this change was due to the thick canopy of shade that hung above, Alice and Analeigh couldn't help but feel as though there was a touch of the supernatural involved, while Davey tried not to think about it whatsoever. He still held stubborn doubt that the witch – Mother Bombalan – was anything more than a local legend and a convenient scapegoat used (often humorously) by the people who lived in the town below. If a car was a lemon, a sports team was to lose, or a crop was to fail, it was usually blamed on Mother Bombalan. When Davey was younger he had been prone to nightmares and following the dare that sent him to look upon the hut, Bombalan had become heavily featured in these nocturnal terrors. In his sleep he had conjured green skin, pointed hat, and endless warts. The smokestack he'd witnessed became a cauldron boiling over fire and filled with children who had seen things they shouldn't have. But as he had grown the nightmares had become less common and he had reassured himself that the hut had simply fallen to squatters and that the smoke was evidence of a transient, nothing more.

Alice, however, had always believed that the witch and her magic were real. She believed hexes were possible, love potions were obtainable, and that there was (within everything) far more than meets the eye. There was no doubt in her mind that there was strange magic in the woods and the reality of Ryan's ghost – while horrifying – had done nothing but strengthen these convictions. Feeling a keen sense of excitement to meet someone so connected with nature and the cosmos as Bombalan must be, Alice walked with a spring in her step and felt that if anyone had answers about Ryan, it would be the witch.

Analeigh had no such spring in her step and was approaching the situation with quiet reservations and forced optimism. She, like Davey, had quickly grown out of the idea that the forest witch was real and in the six years since having ventured to the hut had convinced herself that the shadow she had seen move across its window could have belonged to anyone. This belief had eroded the moment she had seen Ryan, or what Ryan had become. It wasn't that his existence threatened to redefine her worldview like it had for Davey, but instead that in seeing Ryan she had felt a strange sameness. A cold fear had crept into her body and frozen her heart moments before she had even sighted the ghost, yet it had seemed vaguely familiar. It was however, not until Alice had suggested visiting Mother Bombalan that Analeigh was able to place this fear, and recognise that the last time she had felt it was when, six years earlier, she had looked upon the witch's twisted hut and seen the dark silhouette. This strange recognition had given her private reservations towards Alice's suggestion they visit the witch, but there wasn't much she wouldn't do to help a friend, and seeing no alternative for helping Ryan, she had agreed they should try.

As they followed the unmarked path towards the hut, Davey reflected that the forest was the one place in town that hadn't been decorated for Halloween and was the one place that didn't need to be. Their surroundings were undeniably creepy and he felt the unsettling sensation that they were being watched. Shaking his head, he considered the countless eyes of unseen forest creatures they had no doubt passed, and supposed they likely were. The setting and the situation played on his nerves and, hating that he had become so jumpy, he began attempting to disparage the truth of what he felt. "It's all just a load of crap, you'll see," he muttered unconvincingly.

"If ghosts exist, then surely you agree magic can?" Alice responded.

"Yes," he said hollowly, after a long pause. "But that doesn't mean the witch is real too," he objected, clinging to any chance of normality he could find.

"What about Melvin?" asked Alice, thinking back to how happy the pair had looked on the lawn and in the sun, as they trudged through the dark and the cold.

"What about Melvin?" Davey spat, knowing full well where this was going. "And don't say love potions," he said, attempting to pre-empt it.

"The prettiest girl in school, dating the most Melvin boy in school. If that's not witch's magic, then I don't know what is!"

"Are we talking about Melvin whose dad owns the town bank and Helen who likes designer clothing?" Davey queried in facetious clarification.

"Everyone says Melvin visited the hut," Alice argued, ignoring and possibly forgetting that it was she who had first suggested that the love potion had come from the witch.

"They do say he bought a love potion," agreed Analeigh, more to further stir up Davey than from actual conviction.

"They say his dad owns a boat," he countered dryly.

"What use would a boat be, we're surrounded by forest?" laughed Alice, who, spotting the clearing, pointed towards the dark structure.

73

Davey led the group from the treeline into the clearing with false bravado, but as he drew closer to the hut his strides quickly turned into short, reluctant steps. The hut was about the size of a small classroom and seemed as though it tilted forward and looked down upon them. It was built entirely of black rotten wood, its roof was pointed and its windows dark with curtains drawn. At its front stood an old wooden door that sat atop three small and uneven steps, with a hand-scrawled note that read, OPEN.

"Do we knock?" asked Alice.

"I think we just go in – like a store," said Analeigh.

"A store that sells love potions?" Alice smiled.

Davey sighed, mounted the creaking steps and pushed through the entrance. The door groaned loudly and a bell above chimed to announce their presence.

Everything that surrounded them within the structure was shelves, bookcases, and cabinets – not a single surface of the hut had gone unused. Books, artifacts, vials, and herbs were stored indiscriminately amongst one another – there appeared to be no organisation or order. At the far end of the room sat an unattended and dusty counter, with a beaded curtain doorway beyond it. Alice's attention was immediately caught by a rod that held several bracelets, each adorned with small, circular silver charms with runic symbols embossed on them. She examined these carefully and curiously, wondering if they were merely pretty decorations or had a greater meaning, while Davey slowly walked away and ran his hand along a dusty shelf of glass jars too grime-covered to see inside. Pausing, he used the sleeve of his shirt to polish one, peered within, then jumped back, startled. The jar held a preserved though deteriorating brain.

"How's that for a Halloween decoration?" he mumbled as he collected himself from the fright.

Leaving the bracelets, Alice came up beside him and examined the jar for herself. "Not unless you want kids throwing up on your porch," she commented in disgust.

"It's just a sheep brain," he summarised dismissively, then added, "I hope."

Analeigh had wandered slightly away from the pair and was looking through a large collection of books that lined the room's western wall. Most were covered in dust and some had begun to rot away. Even amongst the ones that remained intact, none had recognisable titles on their spines.

"Maybe she's not here?" Alice whispered.

"Doesn't she live here?" came the equally quiet response.

"I can't imagine her commuting... but with the size of this room, I don't think this hut has much space left for living quarters," Davey hissed.

Alice walked towards an open glass cabinet, then loudly called out "Look!" causing her two friends to jump. In her hand she held a small curved bottle, which she handed to Davey triumphantly.

Taking the bottle, he squinted at the label, then read aloud in disbelief, "Love potion." Alice smiled. "Well I'll be damned," he conceded. "But that doesn't mean it works."

Before Alice could give a response, the sound of shifting beads drew their attention towards the dusty counter, where their hostess had appeared. She was tall – perhaps unnaturally so, or perhaps just exaggerated by the low ceiling, which she was forced to dip her head and shoulders to avoid. Her limbs were long, thin, and lanky – her fingers seemed to extend in length to meet the items that she reached out to touch. She looked like an accident in taxidermy. Her skin was thin, leathery, and tight, as if someone had used too little material while trying to reupholster an old sofa.

Analeigh instantly feared her.

"You seek Mother Bombalan," the witch stated in a thick European-sounding accent that Davey doubted was real.

"How does she know that?" whispered Alice in awe.

"We're standing in her store," replied Davey. He paused in consideration, then held up the small curved bottle with the label facing towards the strange skeletal woman. "Does this really work?"

The witch smiled a dry grin that cracked her skin and opened small streams of blood along her lips. "It might," she said, "but you're not here for love potions."

"No..." agreed Alice, while Davey slowly lowered the bottle and placed it back into the glass cabinet. "We're here because they say you can do magic and we've encountered something... supernatural," she continued.

"The spirit boy," replied Mother Bombalan, nodding at the surprised gasps and glances shared between Alice and Analeigh.

"Yes. The one from the newspaper," said Davey, refusing to be impressed. "What – " he began, before fully knowing what he would ask. "What is it?"

"A broken spirit – the ghost of a boy. Sometimes when a death is especially traumatic or due to... other circumstances, a soul will become damaged, ripped and torn and missing pieces, trapped between the planes," answered the witch.

"Can you help us?" asked Analeigh. "Can you help him?"

"A ghost is a spirit that has become torn and broken. Like tattered garments this damage can be repaired, but it is difficult and dangerous magic," she said, fixing her gaze on Analeigh.

"Can anyone learn to do it?" asked Alice with excitement.

"Anyone can learn to cook, but few people have what it takes to become chefs. Among you, only this one," replied the witch, still holding Analeigh in her stare.

Alice felt the sting of jealousy, but quickly pinched her own arm to remind herself of why and for whom they were there, while Analeigh shook her head to clear it, feeling as though she had been hypnotised by the woman's strange grey eyes. "I'm – we're not looking to learn magic. We just want help. Can you—will you help him?" she stuttered.

The slender woman broke her gaze, then reached beneath the counter and retrieved a large, black, dust-covered book. The spine was blank and the front bore a strange sigil with words scratched above it. From what Analeigh could see from its upside-down position, the image on the front looked somewhat like the Vitruvian Man (but with too many arms and crossed legs) crucified on an inverted pentagram.

She shivered. There was a strangeness to the book, it seemed to call – or hum – to her. "What is it?" she asked in awe and fear, and uncertain as to whether she herself meant the book or the sigil.

"A book of techniques in the magic of *soul weaving*," answered the witch, flicking through pages. "If I am to repair your friend's spirit, I will have to... refresh myself on some of its more complicated chapters." She paused on a page towards the end of the book that appeared to show a man suspended in mid-air with strange curved lines cutting through him marked with various notations. "Others I will have to learn for the first time."

"So you can do it?" asked Alice excitedly and the witch slammed the book shut, looking her in the eyes as if seeing her for the first time.

"For a price," she confirmed.

"What price?" asked Davey, feeling certain his theory of her being a scam artist was about to be proven true.

The witch smiled and turned her grey eyes on him while her teeth became stained with the blood that trickled from her lips. "What I need is beyond what you will be willing to supply. To fix his spirit, you will have to pay me two thousand dollars and provide me with a soul," she laid out.

Alice let out a nervous giggle, while Analeigh and Davey were outraged.

"Two grand for mumbo jumbo?!" he spat. "What do you even want with that kind of money out here in the woods?!"

The witch shrugged indifferently and opened her arms in gesture. "See these books, these herbs, these items – do you think *mumbo jumbo* is cheap?"

"Surely we can reach... another agreement?" suggested Analeigh, unwilling to lose so easily their best chance of saving Ryan from his endless turmoil.

"I have told you what I need and that you won't pay it," answered the witch as she returned the closed book back beneath the counter, then turned to leave through the beaded curtain. "If you want the ghost gone, bring me my money and bring me a soul," she reiterated while calmly walking away.

Enraged, Analeigh kicked over a small pile of books and swore, while Alice and Davey shared a defeated glance. They waited within the hut for a few moments longer, half expecting her to re-emerge, and then, seeing that she had no intention to do so, left in silence.

The walk from the hut, through the forest, and across the oval wasn't a long one but, burdened by their failure, it felt like an eternity. Melvin and Helen were still on the grass, and waved again as they crossed the oval, but the friends gave no response, deflated and barely aware of the couple's presence.

Alice was fearful of what the witch had demanded and why she would want a soul.

Davey was insulted by her exorbitant price.

And Analeigh, angry at the witch's unwillingness to help and her own failure to secure it, imagined poor Ryan stuck in his death loop and gritted her teeth, determined to find a way to help him, Mother Bombalan be damned.

Monday, October 12th. 11:00am.

After returning to town the three friends went their separate ways and did not meet again until Monday morning recess. While sitting at their bench and table, they quietly unpacked their snacks and looked extremely tired. Each of them had struggled to sleep Saturday and Sunday night, and it was no longer just Analeigh that was suffering from nightmares of Ryan.

Alice was the first to break the silence. "A human soul," she voiced flatly and in total disbelief. Within her books there were countless examples of deals with the devil and ungodly trades performed at crossroads or in cemeteries, but it had always been with the light side of magic that she had been obsessed, and this unexpected brush with the Satanic frightened her greatly.

"Two grand," answered Davey, who was paid little more than pocket money at his father's hardware store and saw this as an equally unattainable price.

"Do you think she was joking about the soul?" asked Alice, ignoring Davey.

"I really don't," replied Analeigh, remembering with a shudder the strange feeling Bombalan's cold grey eyes had given her.

"She wants us to give her some kind of human sacrifice, a payment in blood... we can't do that, not even for Ryan," Alice lamented.

"She didn't say human, specifically," said Davey before he could stop the thought from slipping out.

Alice shot him a disgusted look and he met her eyes, then quickly looked away feeling adequately chastised.

"We're not killing *anything*. We'll find another way," answered Analeigh firmly.

"Besides," added Alice, "as much as I love animals, Bombalan wanted a soul... and... well, I do love animals but most of my books – and the *Bible* – they seem to think animals don't have those."

Cruel laughter broke in on their discussion as it drifted over from the school buildings and the trio looked up to see that Cole, having tripped a student three years his junior, was guffawing obnoxiously. The kid struggled back onto his feet and just as he regained balance, Cole pushed him over again, then was himself dragged away with the strap of his backpack by a furious teacher.

"If she really wants a human soul, we could give her Cole's, that is, if we can find it." suggested Analeigh jokingly.

"Not funny," protested Alice.

"A little funny," conceded Davey.

The three fell silent again and didn't speak further until they had finished their snacks and drinks.

The bell rang and Analeigh stood, took two steps, then paused and turned. "Do you really think she could have done anything about it?" she asked quietly.

"... yes," said Alice after a hesitant pause.

"Davey?" asked Analeigh, who valued his analytical approach even if it often annoyed and deflated her.

"Well…" he said, collecting his thoughts. "As you pointed out earlier, last week I would have said that ghosts aren't real and yet – so yeah, I think maybe the creepy old bat really does have some kind of useful ghost-removal powers… or at the very least I admit it's not impossible." He paused, then added, "I still think that two grand is too much."

Most students had already begun to leave the oval and funnel their way back into the classrooms, but Alice, Davey, and Analeigh refused to move from their positions while such a serious discussion was taking place.

"We all agree that we can't just leave Ryan having to go through… *that* every night," Analeigh outlined, making sure that they each were on the same page.

"Yes," said Davey and glanced sideways towards Alice, who nodded. They both knew exactly how Analeigh felt, but with no money and no will to cross such a dark line, found themselves unsure of what exactly could be done.

"So we are committed to doing what it takes." Analeigh parsed as a statement rather than a question.

"Ani, we can't give the witch a human soul," said Alice softly.

"I know that!" spat Analeigh.

"And we don't have two grand," added Davey.

"I know that too," she sighed.

"So what do you suggest?" asked Alice.

Analeigh began to pace and formulate her plan. "We saw the book – the one that Bombalan would need for the spell," she mused.

"I don't think you'll find it in the local library," answered Davey uneasily. He glanced down at his watch and saw that he was already two minutes late for maths class, but was unwilling to be the first to move.

"We don't need it to be in the library, we already know where a copy is. We know that Mother Bombalan has one and we know that she keeps it under the counter," continued Analeigh, speaking slowly.

Davey's mouth fell open, and Alice physically started at the suggestion. "You don't mean—"

"—I do," interrupted Analeigh.

"I don't like where this is going," Davey grumbled.

"You agreed that we should do what it takes to help Ryan," Analeigh reminded him.

"Just to be clear – to get this out in the complete open – you are suggesting that we *steal* the book from Mother Bombalan... is that right?" he asked.

It was exactly what Analeigh was suggesting, but hearing it come from someone else made her see just how crazed and brazen it sounded. Even so, seeing no other possible alternative, she swallowed heavily and gave a nod in confirmation.

"Great, so we become thieves and piss off someone who apparently has magical powers!" said Davey, sarcasm mixing with hysteria. "And once we've got the book, then what?"

"The witch – Mother Bombalan – she said *I* could perform magic," replied Analeigh uneasily.

"No, she didn't," he countered.

"She did heavily imply it. Or that she could learn it..." whispered Alice, recalling her strong jealousy over Analeigh's supposed ability. At this Davey shot Alice an annoyed glance and, seeing his disapproval, she hastened to add, "But you *don't* know how to do magic, Ani."

"Neither does Bombalan – or at least, not that kind of magic, remember? She herself said she would have to study the book before she could help Ryan!"

"She *said* that the magic was very difficult and dangerous," Davey warned.

"Sure, but she said she could learn it *from the book*."

"She did say that," said Alice quietly, receiving another angry glare from Davey and an appreciative smile from Analeigh. "Both of those things – book learning and dangerous," she quickly clarified.

"So, we steal the book," said Analeigh, doubling down.

"I don't like this plan," said Davey, standing to face Analeigh directly while Alice, still seated, shrank back from the argument. "What if we get caught and then there's police involvement? Or if we do succeed in stealing it, then what if it turns out she's a fraud and the book does nothing for us?!"

"And what if we don't get caught, and magic is real, and the book is exactly what we need to help Ryan?" countered Analeigh.

"Then maybe that's the worst outcome of all, because if magic turns out to be real, then we've stolen from a witch!"

"We owe it to Ryan to take that risk."

"Do we?!"

The two of them were at a standstill, until Alice placed a hand on Davey's arm to break the tension. "He would have done the same for us," she said softly.

"Should we put it to a vote?" Analeigh offered.

Their most difficult and controversial decisions had always been put to a vote and in the decade and a half the three of them had been friends, the results of such a vote had never been rejected. Davey, however, saw little point in running the matter through such a process. It was clear to him, without any votes cast, that the outcome would be against him.

"No," he finally answered. "We'll do it your way, but I'm going on record saying that I was in favour of *not* pissing off the possibly magical, likely Satanic, forest witch."

"So noted," answered Analeigh.

"Fine," he said, staring past her towards the classrooms where their lessons had already begun without them. "When are we doing this?"

Analeigh looked across the oval and into the forest. "Friday night," she declared. "Like you said, it didn't look like there was enough room inside the hut for living quarters and if it is just her store, then there's a good chance it will be empty after dark."

Davey swallowed hard. He didn't like the idea of going into the forest at night, but couldn't fault her logic. "Friday," he reluctantly agreed.

Monday, October 12th. 3:45pm.

After school ended on Monday, Davey immediately committed himself to his new branch of self-education, which – much to his disgust – consisted largely of a growing number of books on mysticism, spiritualism, and the occult. If these things were real (as he was begrudgingly beginning to accept, they were) then he wanted the fullest understanding of them he could possibly obtain. Unsurprisingly, books focused on the occult were few and far between in a public school library and in short order he had read everything his school had to offer on the subjects. Once the library was exhausted he had gone to Alice who lent him any of her books that she herself had already committed to memory. Then with Alice tagging along he visited various new and used bookstores throughout Clarke Valley, spending some of his hard-earned money from the hardware store on obtaining further volumes that could not otherwise be borrowed.

With his fast-growing collection, Davey continued to structure and restructure for himself an attempted coherent belief that lined up with what he now knew of the world and with frustration found that few texts seemed to ever agree with one another. With each piece of information he learned, several older pieces would need to be discarded in order for it to logically fit. It wasn't just that science disagreed with religion, or that mysticism disagreed with philosophy, but that even within each discipline supposed authorities on any subject disagreed with one another. He had read compelling arguments for the mind that resulted in conclusions both for and against the soul, had seen endless suggestions about what a spirit was or wasn't and where it went after death if anywhere, and learned that everything from the beginning of the universe to the actions of a molecule were in dispute.

His ordered world had become chaos and with an increasing feeling of defeat Davey was not shocked to find that no two books on the existence or nature of ghosts agreed on their form, motivation, or substance. When he discussed these inconsistencies with Alice, he marvelled over how she couldn't see why these contradictions were of concern to him, and scolded himself for finding that he longed to have such a non-critical approach. With each passing day he felt more disoriented and uncertain with the world than he had ever before been and with a slight headache he wished for the days when he could see an issue and form a single coherent conviction.

Thursday, October 15th. 3:00am.

Analeigh slept in peace and calmness, and as she did, she dreamed.

In her dream she walked the winding path of Hansen Road under the midday Moon, but no longer did she suffer its sticky surface. Like before she came upon the old man who aged backwards as he sank until eventually becoming her friend, but no longer was he doomed to drown.

With a strong hand and long fingers, Analeigh saw herself reaching down to the swallowing bitumen just as only Ryan's hand and head were left visible. She felt strong and powerful, and saw herself pulling Ryan out of the blackness until she held him high above her head, while the raven-branched trees remained quiet and undisturbed. She let him go and marvelled as he remained suspended in mid-air – still and beautiful. He floated, sprouted wings of his own, soared off high above the treeline to the midday Moon, and became but a speck against its glow. As he shrank and disappeared beyond sight, Analeigh waved him goodbye, while the ravens watched and glared.

Then she awoke – not with a start, but with a calm feeling of serenity.

It had only been since Monday night – after she had outlined her plans to steal the book – that her dreams had begun to shift in tone. At first her dreamself had only partially succeeded, but the ravens had beat their wings and Ryan had fallen to the earth, limp and dead. As the week continued, each night she made progress. Tonight, however, was the first time that it had been a total success and she could not imagine a better omen.

Wrapped in this calm reassurance, she rolled over and, for the first time in weeks, easily fell back asleep.

Friday, October 16th. 2pm.

In maths class Alice sat and read one of the several authentic-looking hardback tomes she had bought with Davey from an old bookstore Monday afternoon. The book had a pentagram on its cover and was now amongst the growing few in her collection that focused entirely on the dark side of magic. She had circled passages on hexes, and underlined sentences on curses, and discovered that a familiar was not merely a pet. There was no talk of meditation or good vibes in this book and no longer was she merely learning for the sake of learning.

Instead, she was preparing for their encounter.

Tonight they would be crossing a witch who would conceivably want to seek vengeance against them, and with each chapter Alice read, she learned, and was paled by the extensive details the book provided on the many horrible ways Bombalan may try to do so. There was talk of boils, and hair loss, and disease and, as she turned a page and continued to ignore her classroom lesson, she gasped, and squinted at the illustrations she had found.

At the top of the page the chapter was marked "Protective charms against hexes and curses" and dead centre – surrounded by dozens of other illustrations – were the small runes she had seen on silver charm bracelets within Bombalan's hut. She traced her finger over the images and read about how such charms would protect their wearers from magical ill intention, and made sure to commit their designs to memory. The charms were the first bit of positivity she had found within the dark books that had occupied her week, yet despite this she remained in agreement with Analeigh that they must do whatever it took to help Ryan. It would be dangerous, she did not doubt that, but Analeigh was right about them needing to try. And now, with the small possibility of protection this book offered, she held out a glimmer of hope that they might just get away with their plan unscathed.

Despite this modicum of hope, when passing the broken railing on her way back down the hill towards her home for their weekly sleepover, she shuddered, and knew that she now feared magic more than she had ever loved it.

Friday, October 16th. 11pm.

The three friends sat in Alice's small bedroom with open boxes of barely eaten pizza, while on the TV an energetic skeleton introduced the night's first film, *Fiend Without a Face*. With their minds dwelling on their evening plans, they found they had little appetite and hardly noticed when the host finished talking and the movie began. Several shots of an airforce base played out before them on the TV's small black and white screen and a soldier stood near a forest looking on edge. It was less than two minutes into the film, before even the title screen had come up, when Alice's bedside alarm clock went off, causing the friends to jump and signaling that it was time to sneak out into the forest for their intended larceny.

The trio hadn't waited until near midnight this time, but only until they were sure that Alice's father had gone to bed. By 11:15pm they were out the door, in the car and winding their way back up Hansen Road, past the broken barrier and towards the student parking lot of Clarke Valley High.

The short drive was charged with nervous energy.

Once they arrived, Alice, Davey, and Analeigh hastened across the oval. They held their torches in hand but kept them turned off, allowing the brightness of the Moon to steer them. As they crossed into the thick vegetation of the forest, this light source was quickly lost. The stars and the Moon were swallowed by the overhead canopy of leaves and branches, and the evening was thrown into blackness. At night, the forest seemed boundless, cruel and twisted: the trees were taller, further gnarled and denser. Within five metres of entering the forest, darkness ruled and their torches were switched on.

The forest was silent – eerily so – and soon the friends found themselves feeling as though they had to speak, not out of companionship but to drown out the crypt-like silence, which somehow felt both vast and claustrophobic.

"Have you ever been here at night? You know, aside from…" Davey trailed off, trying his best to avoid mentioning their horrific encounter with Ryan's ghost on the road somewhere south-east of their position.

"At night? No, never," responded Alice.

"It doesn't feel safe," he whispered, as though they might be overheard.

"I've never heard of bears or anything in these parts," replied Analeigh, fully aware that this was not what Davey feared.

The trio fell quiet again and continued to trudge over rocks, thick tree roots and unexpected dips. The path to the witch's hut was an unofficial one and its uneven and unkept nature became increasingly evident in the night's darkness. With only their torches for guidance, they discovered that despite having gone to Bombalan's hut only a week before, getting turned around was easy and they had to backtrack on several occasions.

"So what do you – I mean – *we* plan to do when we get there?" Davey asked, realising that beyond stealing Bombalan's book, they hadn't actually formulated a plan for the burglary.

"Let ourselves in, get the book from under the counter, leave in a hurry," Analeigh mechanically listed.

"What makes you think her door won't be locked?" he asked, surprised that he hadn't considered the possibility earlier.

"No one locks their doors in Clarke Valley," Alice chimed in, then with a more serious tone added, "let alone scary witches who own secluded forest huts."

"Yeah," agreed Analeigh. "I doubt it'll be locked."

Because no one in their right mind would steal from a spooky secluded witch, Davey thought, but kept to himself.

All that they had brought with them were the three torches and a single backpack slung over Analeigh's shoulder. This was her schoolbag that she had been using since Year 2 and it was identical to any other schoolbag purchased from the uniform store that year albeit for the word *Analeigh* scribbled across the back in fading black Texta. They had no weapons, no flares and no medical supplies if things were to go south on them. For a moment Davey allowed himself to consider how absurd it was that he and his two schoolfriends were in a forest at night, planning to burglarise a witch, but his contemplations were shattered when Analeigh firmly announced, "We're here."

They walked into the clearing and raised their torches towards the hut, tracing the old structure and bringing into view its warped wood and haphazard repairs, until finally their lights met and settled on the wooden door. There was no longer an OPEN sign and the hut seemed even less inviting than it had the previous weekend.

"It... looks bigger during the night," commented Davey.

"I feel smaller during the night," replied Alice.

"What if she *does* live here?" he whispered, but received no response.

It had been Analeigh's idea and so, taking the initiative, she led the way up the three small steps towards the door and lightly pushed it open, the entrance-bell chiming. Davey had half-wished for it to be locked, forcing them to turn back, and swore when it opened with ease, while Alice let out a long breath that she didn't realise she had been holding. "Come on," Analeigh whispered.

Not pausing to look for a light switch, they entered the store using their torches to guide them. There was no wasting time. None of them wished to be there for a moment longer than necessary. Immediately Alice split off from the group and found her way to the wooden rod on which the charm bracelets hung, sliding free three that each bore the runes she had memorised.

"What are you doing? We're not here to steal jewellery," hissed Davey, barely believing what he was seeing.

"These are charm bracelets," Alice whispered back. "They should protect us from magical ill intention."

She passed one to each of her friends and Davey could not put his on fast enough. They then continued through the store, past the assorted oddities and towards the counter. Analeigh was the first to reach it. Placing her hand under the benchtop, she blindly felt around, then retrieved the book and thumped it down onto the counter with more force than she had intended. A loud *thwack* echoed out of the hardback volume and various trinkets on the countertop jingled and jangled while dust disturbed by the collision flew away from the book and Analeigh sucked in air through her teeth. Alice and Davey both instinctively jumped at the noise, then locked eyes with one another. Slowly they glanced away and around the room, finally focusing their pupils down onto the book.

"Is... is that the right one?" asked Alice.

Analeigh carelessly opened the tome to about two-thirds of the way in, its bulk still making a soft *thud* on the table as it fell open. Staring up at them was the strange depiction of a figure she had glimpsed the last time they were here. The illustration showed a man suspended in mid-air with what appeared to be white ribbons flying from his veins, nostrils and arms. The ribbons continued to twist downwards and back into a second figure previously obscured by Bombalan's hand which stood on the ground. This was undoubtedly the page Analeigh had seen earlier, but now that she was closer, she could see further details. There were long handwritten paragraphs penned in small cramped cursive, accompanied by looser scratchings that had obviously been written by a second hand. The sentences were full of words that she did not recognise and she found herself unsure whether it was slipping into other languages, archaic English or unfamiliar technical terms – later she guessed that it was a mixture of all three. Underneath these tangled paragraphs were vibrantly coloured runes of simple design that reminded Analeigh of a book she had once read on the Aztecs. Softly she closed the book and looked upon the strange Vitruvian Man pentagram sigil on the front cover, above which – as if with a nail – the words 'Soul Weaver' had been scratched. "Yes," she said, "this is *definitely* the book."

With nervous haste Davey reached over, snapped up the book and forced it into Analeigh's hands. "Good, then take it and let's now please go," he hissed with urgency, feeling that they were already pushing their luck.

She nodded and they began tracing their way back past the cluttered shelves of peculiarities and out the small store. Standing on the uppermost step, she carefully closed the door behind them, the bell chimed, and all three let out a collective sigh.

Immediately Davey felt on edge. "Listen," he whispered.

Frogs were croaking, owls were hooting and a breeze blew through the leaves, creaking the branches.

"You hear it?"

"Birds, toads, the wind?" ventured Alice.

"*Noise*. Before, there wasn't any," answered Analeigh.

Unsettled, the friends warily descended the bottom two steps.

Back on solid ground in the clearing, Analeigh unslung her backpack and deposited their prize within, making sure to zip the bag fully closed to ensure the book's safety. She stood up, shifted the weight of the bag back onto her shoulders and then jumped as a violent scream rang out from behind them. They turned and instinctively darted their torches towards the source of the noise. Expecting to see the witch – vengeful and understandably angry – the trio were surprised to find that instead, perched atop the pointed roof of the wooden shack, was a raven of seemingly unnatural size.

Alice muttered quietly and in terror something about "familiars".

The raven looked to Davey to be twice the size of a regular bird – but things often look larger in the dark, he quickly reassured himself.

It wasn't until the bird screamed a second time that they realised the forest had once again fallen silent. And then it swooped.

The raven moved soundlessly in the blackness and cut talons of red blood across Davey's cheek. He screamed and slapped his hand to his face, but the raven was already back atop its perch on the old woodland hut. Davey yelled out again, this time in anger at the bird – and his scream was immediately drowned out as the raven screamed in return.

"It's Bombalan's familiar!" cried Alice with certainty and, as though the raven had understood, it dived towards her, talons out.

This time the three friends successfully ducked the attack and the raven was back atop the old hut.

"What do we do?" asked Davey, turning to Alice in acknowledgement of her greater understanding of such things.

Her mind raced. She had been reading all about familiars and their relationships with witches over the last week, but in horror realised that nothing she had read gave her much insight into what to do when attacked by one.

"Alice?" Analeigh prompted with urgency and the raven screamed again.

"Run?" Alice suggested simply.

"Run!" agreed Analeigh and Davey.

They sprinted back out of the hut's small clearing and into the treeline, hearing the bird screech behind them and feeling oddly comforted by the dark cover the trees provided. Their torches bounced erratically in their hands, the lights darting around them without direction, and the friends ran blind and in fear.

Without warning, Analeigh felt a rush of air burst across the back of her neck, followed by a hard collision against her schoolbag. Knocked off her feet, she crashed to the forest floor and felt certain that – for maybe just a moment – she had been airborne. She stood and looked around, but could see no other torch lights in the darkness that surrounded her.

She had been separated.

The scream echoed again through the trees, though she could not tell from which direction, and before she had even realised what was happening, she was knocked to her knees once more.

Analeigh had to get out of this forest. She knew this for a fact. She knew that it was a matter of life and death.

Her sprint started as a crawl, then she was running as fast as her lungs and legs would allow. She paid no heed to the leaves and branches that scratched at her face and tore at her clothes. As she ran, she heard distant screams followed by nearby blasts of air, but she kept her footing and suddenly burst through the treeline, finding herself staring at gravelled road and broken guardrail.

Deep in the forest behind her and impossibly far away, she heard the scream of the raven fade into the distance. In front of her, she heard scrapes and thuds, and a mournful, pitiable moan.

It was midnight and the ghost of Ryan Crosnor was right on time.

He moved with the jangled wrongness of a puppet with tangled strings and, while it hadn't been obvious when she had seen his ghost from within the car, there was a smell about him. It was positively septic.

"I'm sorry, Ryan," she whispered, a tear rolling down her cheek.

His foot dragged as he moved across the road and the exposed bones of his ankle's compound fracture made rough scraping noises.

"I'm sorry," she said again and the creature moaned sadly.

He reached halfway across the pavement, then his transparent figure met with the beam from her torch and vanished.

"I *will* find a way to help you," she promised, before turning and beginning her walk up the long, winding road.

By foot, it was a 15-minute uphill trudge from the point of the fatal accident to the school parking lot. On arrival, she found her friends pacing back and forth in front of Davey's car, torches in hand, arguing about whether they should re-enter the forest in search of her or call the police. The side of Davey's face and his collar were soaked in blood.

They hugged and cried tears of relief, then got into the car and started the journey back towards town. As they descended the hill, Analeigh filled them in on what had happened when they were split up, pausing her recollection only as they passed the broken barrier. They all agreed that Alice was correct and that the raven was a servant of the witch, Bombalan, if not the witch herself.

Back in the warm safety of Alice's room, Analeigh helped bandage Davey's face and the trio again broke out Claire's picture books and read until daylight while Claire slept soundly in her own room, unaware that her sister had ever left the house or that her library had once more been pilfered.

"Expecting to see the witch — vengeful and understandably angry — the trio were surprised to find that instead, perched atop the pointed roof of the wooden shack, was a raven of seemingly unnatural size."

Part 3: The Witch

Saturday, October 17th. 9:30am.

With Analeigh eager to begin study of the book and Davey having to go to work, both friends left Alice's home before she had woken. For Analeigh, sleep had come easily following the horrors of the raven; there had been no nightmares and there had been no dreams of the sticky road or the midday Moon. She credited this sound sleep to their positive change in prospects. With the book now in their possession, she found herself increasingly confident they would be able to repair Ryan's broken spirit and free him from his death loop on Hansen Road. *Provided you can actually learn magic!* an inner voice cruelly criticised, but quickly she shook her head to clear it.

Pulling her car alongside the kerb that ran out front her house, she exited the vehicle, and walked towards the front door, past the foam-cut gravestones and plastic skeletons that decorated the lawn. Today was going to be a *good* day, and today was going to be a *successful* day and, as she let herself into the house, she was determined to make these plans of success a reality. Not bothering with breakfast or a shower, she greeted her mother with a kiss on the cheek, then ran straight upstairs to her bedroom. Opening the book on her desk, she was immediately hit with a waft of musty air that attested to the tome's age and, stifling a sneeze, she scanned her eyes over the strange markings and striking pictograms found within.

The cursive might as well have been in another language and Analeigh found herself uncertain that it wasn't. Straining her eyes against the overly loopy letters that leaned as though they had suffered through an earthquake, she attempted to separate them from one another in her mind. A stylised L, she found, could just as easily have been a lazy A, while spaces between words expanded and narrowed to extreme and uneven degrees. In some sections her thumb could comfortably fit between two groups of letters, whereas in others they were strung together and unbroken for a full line of the text. Sometimes a word would stand out – usually written in block letters – and Analeigh would circle it, then wonder at its possible significance. By the end of the first page she had circled nine such words amongst the tangled mess of writing, but with no further context to ground them failed to understand their meaning or importance. When attempting to look these words up in her small pocket dictionary, she discovered they were not featured and reasoned they must be archaic and unknown to modern English.

Abandoning the scribbled text as inescapably illegible, Analeigh turned her attention to the bright runic pictograms that accompanied each paragraph. Remembering having learned about the Rosetta Stone in history class, she considered whether this text, like the stone, might contain content repeated in several different languages. Inspired by this theory, she began to scrutinise the images closely, hoping they might stand as a secondary translation for the unreadable text. The runes that ran beneath the first paragraph of tangled incomprehension depicted a small cube in the distance and a detailed hand in the foreground. From left to right, she realised that the pictograms read like a comic and showed the hand twisting into various shapes and the cube hovering towards its open palm. The runes were self-explanatory enough and she immediately understood them to be a guide on how to perform some form of telekinesis. With a furrowed brow, she extended her hand and fumbled through a rough approximation of the hand positions shown in the diagram. While at first appearing simple, in practise several felt cramped, unnatural, and decidedly uncomfortable. Upon completing the cycle, she found that nothing had happened.

She frowned, and tried again, and frowned once more.

Standing up from her desk, Analeigh slowly paced the room, then stopped upon sighting a colourful Rubik's cube that sat on her bookshelf. For a moment she was reminded that Ryan had been able to solve the Rubik's cube in under three minutes, but with effort refocused herself back onto the task at hand. She then considered that she, unlike the hand depicted in the diagram, had been performing the movements of her fingers with no target for her intended powers to manipulate. Realising that this may have been the issue, she took the cube back to her desk, placed it down as shown in the pictograms, and set to attempting the movements once more.

Halfway through her motions, the colourful cube started to vibrate and Analeigh gasped in surprise – breaking her concentration and causing the cube to resume its inanimate existence.

She tried again, this time ignoring the shaking of the cube and maintaining her focus on her hand movements. The cube shook and danced a little, but did not move toward her palm like the pictures suggested it should.

Frowning, she redirected her focus back to the runes, and with deliberate slowness repeated the movements, attempting to copy each of them individually, exactly as they were shown. In some positions her fingers were expected to bend at awkward angles that felt painful and difficult to hold, and she started to wish that she were double-jointed. A straightened index finger was expected to shift so that it was bent at the second knuckle yet straight at the first. Naturally it wished to curve at the first and this small intricacy alone took a good twenty minutes to master. After hours of trying these strange positions, a dull ache was developing in the palm of her hand and her fingers throbbed as though they had been caught in a door. Despite this, by 2pm she had reached a level of proficiency in which she was able to perfectly replicate each of the specific hand positions shown throughout the six runes.

Now, with her attention back onto the cube, she strung the positions together, her hand flowing through the movements once more. Like learning a song on a musical instrument, they had become muscle-memory and her fingers snapped easily from one to another without thought or effort. Despite this, the bright cube remained static, no longer even shaking, and after minutes of failure she shifted her attention back to the book and her hand, hoping to verify that her positions were correct. They were, and she continued to cycle and shift concentration from her hand to the cube and back, until eventually she turned her thoughts inward.

Her introspection focused on her breathing, her pulse, and her energy. Energy that until now Analeigh had never before felt, but immediately recognised as always having been there – dormant – like a secondary self that moved in time with the rest of her being. Her hand cycled through the positions and she breathed and concentrated on this energy form that stretched out from her – like a phantom limb – and extended beyond the physical barrier of her hand towards the cube. It encompassed the cube and bathed it in her life force, and she could feel the object in a way that was deeper than her sense of touch would have allowed.

Her hand continued to cycle through the positions and the cube lifted off the desk from half a metre away, and Analeigh could feel its weight – not in terms of grams, but in terms of the shared matter that was both the cube and herself, and the space between them that made up the universe.

Her hand cycled and snapped and popped, and the cube floated towards her, until eventually it dropped into her outstretched palm and Analeigh let out a shaky breath, realising that her forehead was soaked in sweat.

A wave of relief washed over her as though a weight had been lifted from her consciousness. The feeling was not unlike what one might experience minutes after exoneration following an especially awkward church confessional – but there was something more to it than that. It wasn't just that she experienced power or the satisfaction of doing something that weeks earlier she would have considered a miracle – there was, to the ritual, a strangely addictive nature. There was a physical element that gave an easing of tensions, relaxed her body, and invoked euphoria. In a way the experience felt somewhat masturbatorial, yet wholly unsexual. She immediately moved the cube further away and began again the cycle of hand gestures and, as the energy outstretched, she felt the same relief and pleasure, and she placed back the cube once and twice more until eventually she moved on to the second paragraph of text and its accompanying pictograms.

Quickly Analeigh realised that learning magic to help Ryan was not only the right thing to do.

It also felt great.

Monday, October 19th. 8:10am.

By the time the weekend was over Alice had barely managed to begin to study for her biology exam, Davey had sold several dozen hammers, a wheelbarrow, and enough timber to build a deck, and Analeigh had mastered roughly one-third of the book's mystical runes. Despite this, like most weekends it had felt too short and before anyone could do so much as blink an eye, Monday had arrived.

In a rare display of punctuality, Analeigh – eager to show off what she had learned – was the first at school and sat waiting for her friends before they had even left their homes. She tapped her foot in anticipation and felt that she could hardly wait to see the expression on Davey's once-sceptical face or the reaction from the long-time magically obsessed Alice. As they finally pulled their cars into student parking and walked over to join her at their usual spot, she excitedly retrieved a large marble from her pocket, placed it on the table, then glanced around to ensure that no other students were near enough to see. Once satisfied, she began to display her newfound talents. In awe, Davey and Alice leaned in and watched closely.

"I started with the smaller stuff," she explained, running her hand in circles above the wooden table as the glass ball kept pace below. "Moving things, spinning pinwheels and such." She pulled her hand further away and the small ball lifted off from the rough wooden surface, hovering to maintain the distance. Turning her hand upwards, the ball silently moved towards it, and settled in her palm.

"Holy shit," whispered Davey.

"But, but how is it done? You've not said any... magical words or anything..." stuttered Alice as her mind rushed over the seemingly endless texts she had read on the use of magic.

Pausing, Analeigh considered the question, while Davey stared at the marble in her palm with stunned, resigned acceptance. Over the last few weeks it had seemed as though each day his worldview was further shattered. While at first this had been terrifying and jarring, it now evoked in him nothing more than a vague numbness. His eyes wandered away from the ball and towards a group of students who laughed as they passed by on the way to their lockers. Reflexively his hand moved to his cheek and traced over the large scab that ran its length. The students laughed again and moved indoors, and he found himself nostalgic for their carefree ignorance. As Analeigh began to answer Alice's question, he listened and tried to shake off his melodramatic contemplations.

"No, no magic words. It's sort of like an energy – there's a flow to it and you can direct it with your movements. I couldn't feel it at first... I guess it's like wiggling your nose, some people can just sort of do it?"

And some just can't, thought Alice bitterly, then caught herself and, attempting to hide her jealousy, asked if

Analeigh thought she would be able to use the book to help Ryan.

"Yes. And soon," came the answer. "But I'm only one third of the way through the book right now – and what looks like the magic needed to heal spirits is pretty near the end. The technique looks kind of advanced, so it will probably still be some days before I get to it... Friday, maybe."

This shook Davey from his mood and washed him with concern. "You've read through one third of the book already? Isn't that kind of rushing things?"

"Mostly read," answered Analeigh awkwardly. "Well, I haven't really *read* any of it, so to speak. It's all very 'ye olde English' and most of the writing is so clumped together that I can't make anything of it. But it comes with diagrams that show body movements and I've been experimenting with those..." She trailed off at the sight of Alice's and Davey's mounting expressions of concern.

"Is this something you should really be *experimenting* with?" he demanded.

"What if the writing has warnings in it?" asked Alice, joining the chorus.

"Like I said," answered Analeigh patiently, "I've only been trying the smaller stuff and when you do it right, well, you *feel* it and when you don't do it right – nothing happens. It isn't like this marble would explode if I messed up trying to make it move, it just wouldn't move."

The others still looked unconvinced, so she gave them a reassuring smile, dropped her palm out from under the ball and twitched her fingers to keep the glass sphere suspended in mid-air. The display of skill worked to distract Alice and Davey from their argument, and they both fell silent and resumed watching in wonderment. After a few seconds, she brought up her other hand and plucked the ball from the sky.

"Incredible," breathed Alice, jealousy replaced by awe.

"Not incredible enough," Analeigh shrugged. "If I'm going to fix Ryan's spirit by this Friday, I'm going to need to study the book every night until then."

"You don't – What I mean to say is... Friday is just a self-imposed deadline. If you're not ready by then, well – I think you should still take this slowly," pained Davey, desperately attempting to ensure his headstrong friend followed sensible precautions.

"I'll be careful," Analeigh assured him. "But I want to do this quickly. I don't want Ryan to suffer any longer than he has to and we don't know if Bombalan has realised that her book is missing yet. Maybe her bird told her... if that's something birds can do... Either way, she might try to get the book back and I want to have learned all that I can before that happens."

Alice thought about the giant winged familiar and shuddered with residual fear, then glanced down at her bracelet and its silver charm. "I think we're safe from Bombalan or at least from her magic – the bracelets seem to be doing their job... I think. I half-expected to wake up with warts or some kind of horrible rash the morning after we stole the book, but I've... well, there's been no fallout, right?" she asked, glancing at her friends for confirmation.

"Speak for yourself," mumbled Davey, touching the red scab that ran along his cheek. He had told his father that he'd gotten the injury from a rosebush, but his father, not believing him, had given a long lecture about getting into fights at school.

"Well, aside from your cheek..." Alice conceded, "but that wasn't directly from her magic, I guess? I mean, the bracelets won't stop her from physically searching us out and taking the book away through non-magical means."

Davey frowned. He had not considered that Mother Bombalan might simply try to take back the book with physical force and briefly wondered whether she had been watching them from the treeline, then dismissed the thought as pointless. If Bombalan was going to try to take back the book, then there was nothing much they could do until she did, and at least a physical attack was something they could see and try to prevent. The idea of her using magic against them concerned him more and he was just glad that the bracelets either worked, or that she had so far left them alone.

As Analeigh resumed performing small tricks, he watched, and slowly started to realise that it wasn't even specifically Bombalan's magic that was worrying him, but rather the nature of magic in general. It wasn't that he thought what Analeigh was doing *was* dangerous, but that he had no idea whether or not it *could* be. He had no concept of how it was she was able to do what she was doing, and felt that her actions were entering into a kind of unknown with potential consequences that were entirely impossible to predict. He watched as his friend continued to manipulate the marble and worried over the means that she managed to do so. She spoke vaguely of feeling an 'energy', but this explanation only concerned him further. There are many kinds of energy in this world, but few that can flow through a human body without causing harm. He thought about electro-shock treatments, and worried about the disruption of neural pathways, and considered the permanent consequences of an electric chair. Then there's the long-term consequences of exposure to unnatural or foreign energies, and he considered how radiation could cause cells to break down and mutate, and cancers to grow. Neither he nor Analeigh knew by what means she was managing to wield these powers, nor the nature of the powers themselves and – much like the existence of ghosts – it was expressly because they were unknown to him that they scared him so greatly.

Before he had time to voice these concerns, the school bell rang and Analeigh pocketed the marble.

As she turned to leave, Davey caught her by the shoulder, and held her firmly. "Just... don't try too much too fast," he pleaded. His mouth opened once more and it

seemed as though he was about to say something further,
but instead it closed and remained silent.

"I'll be careful," she repeated, this time as a promise.

Tuesday, October 20th. 2:15am.

Davey had always been quick to worry. He didn't like to play in tall grass because there might be snakes and he always made sure to bundle up in cold weather. While Analeigh had often goodnaturedly mocked him for these tendencies, she also quietly acknowledged that there were indeed snakes to be found in tall grass and snif-fles to be caught from winter days. When she made her promise about not trying to do too much too fast, she had fully meant what she had said. She respected her friend's opinion and understood his concern, and if he thought she should limit the time she spent practising with the book, then she would endeavour to do so. Despite this, even as she had made the promise there had been a pang of doubt within herself over her ability to abide by it.

As Monday night came and slowly transformed into Tuesday morning, she did her best to put restrictions on the time she spent practising the movements shown within the book. She would study a chapter, then place the book down and tell herself that it was time she did her homework – or that she should go watch TV or maybe read a comic. However, within a few lines of algebra, a few minutes of television or after turning only a few pages of her comic, Analeigh was harassed by a voice in the back of her mind that tugged at her conscience and reminded her of another, earlier promise. A promise made not to Davey on Monday morning, but to Ryan on Friday night. How could she possibly be expected to do maths homework when she could still see Ryan's deformed figure dragging itself across the bitumen every time she closed her eyes? And how could she be expected to read about the adventures of Superman when each practised set of glyphs brought her one step closer to the knowledge necessary to free Ryan from his ghostly suffering? Time and time again throughout the night, she put down, closed or even hid away the strange text, returning to what it was that she should otherwise be doing, and time and time again she found herself pulled back in.

Her subconscious dwelled on it, her consciousness was drawn to it, and her physical practice of the movements were becoming habitual.

She lay in bed with lights out and ran her hand in circles to spin the ceiling fan above. She sat up, and returned to her desk, and read over the glyphs, and retreated back under the covers, then returned once more within mere minutes. She slept and dreamed about mastering the book, and awoke determined to do so.

She doubled down and read new pages of glyphs, then re-read old ones. Her hands were cramped and painful, but she willed them on and continued to practise, fighting through the agony.

Eventually the sun rose on Tuesday morning, and Analeigh splashed water on her tired, pallid face and readied for school. She looked at herself in the mirror and promised her reflection that tonight she would do better – that she would re-establish her sleep schedule, do her

long-neglected homework, and force herself to relax –
but in her bloodshot eyes she could see that even now her
promise lacked conviction. Despite her best intentions,
deep down Analeigh knew that from the moment school
let up, she would once more be studying the book.

Tuesday, October 20th. 1:04pm.

Davey had not paid attention to a word his teacher had said for the whole lesson and was dismayed to see that the stuffy old man intended to continue talking despite lunchbreak having already commenced. The lesson was on geometry – a subject that had held little interest for Davey even before the distracting knowledge of magic had entered his life. As students from the classrooms of more time-focused teachers could be heard already outside, he found that he could concentrate on nothing but the clock. The minute hand appeared static and even the second hand seemed to crawl as the teacher continued to drone. Four minutes into the lunch period, the man finally grumbled something about upcoming tests and home-work, and the class was dismissed. As Davey rushed out of the classroom towards his friends, freedom, and lunch, Cole chased him and fought for acknowledgement.

"I *know* you didn't get it from shaving, Drizzle, you'd have to have gone through puberty first for that!" he teased, pulling beside Davey and matching his pace.

Davey sighed. He should have expected that Cole would make fun of his cut. Briefly he considered lying about its origin, but then decided he couldn't be bothered. "I got it from a bird, Cole... a big one."

"Oh yeah, a bird was it?" Cole whistled. "Was she frustrated you couldn't do it for her? Was it Alice or Ani?" He finished just as they reached the wooden table and Davey, ignoring the comment, slid in beside Alice. "Which of you two birds roughed up Drizzle?" Cole asked with a smile. "Maybe you two would prefer a real man?"

"You'll let us know if you see one," answered Analeigh, not bothering to meet his gaze.

Placing his hand to his forehead like a sailor shielding his eyes, Cole pretended to scan around the schoolyard as though he were searching the horizon. "I see no real men around here," he reported, "but I'm sure to come across a mirror sooner or later."

"Don't cut yourself when it breaks," warned Alice.

"Sure," agreed Cole. "I wouldn't want to end up looking like Drizzle!"

Before Alice could offer another retort, a warning of "Heads up!" was shouted from the oval and a ball flew over as if from out of nowhere. With the reflexes and athleticism that made up for his lack of personality (so far as the Clarke Valley High football team's coach was concerned) Cole caught the ball with little effort. He looked over to where it had come from and saw Jackson and Steven waving. "Go long," he called, threw the ball, then chased after it, leaving the three friends behind.

"Well, I guess he's done with us," commented Davey as they watched the ball getting passed back and forth between the boys.

"Hmm," agreed Alice.

Cole caught another pass, and ran with it, while beneath the wooden table Analeigh's fingers twitched. He ran with the ball and her fingers twitched, and he tripped on his own two feet – his face planting into the dirt. He sat up, coughed, and looked confused.

And Analeigh smiled.

Clarke Valley Gazette. Wednesday, October 21st.

'Police Fail to Nab Ghost During Midnight Manhunt!'

The Hansen Road Poltergeist was spotted once more Monday night, resulting in a three-hour manhunt through the thick forest that surrounds the area.

Police were alerted to the latest sighting by a power-plant worker who claims to have seen a dim figure crawling along the side of the road as he rounded a turn close to midnight. Having heard reports of a ghost, he refused to stop and instead drove down to O'Brien's Bar for a drink. Overhearing the account and fearing that the figure was someone in distress, O'Brien himself called the police to report the incident.

"We don't think there was an injured party there, but with a report like that we have to check it out regardless," Police Chief Braxton told the *Gazette* on Tuesday afternoon. He went on to stress that the search was for an injured person, and not for the ghost or its supposed pranksters. "We didn't expect to find the would-be pranksters hiding in the woods. We knew that by the time we got there, they'd be long gone," he told reporters.

Despite this, Chief Braxton has confirmed that the investigation into the alleged pranks continues and that, when found, those responsible will be prosecuted to the full extent of the law.

Wednesday, October 21st. 11:00am.

By Wednesday, Analeigh had mastered two-thirds of the book. The glyphs she now practised were beyond mere hand movements and she had learned to twist and contort her entire body in a strange kind of mystical dance. She had levitated, she had lightly cut her own finger in order to heal it back over, and she had projected her mind outside of Clarke Valley, far beyond where her physical body had ever travelled. She lost track of time and came to school late, and found it impossible to focus – her mind instead turning to the book that sat on her desk and what she could otherwise be learning had she not come to class.

The importance of her work was further cemented by Wednesday's paper, which reported yet another sighting from Monday night. She read and re-read the article while the teacher droned on unheard at the front of the classroom. When the bell rang, she was excited to head home and resume her study, then disappointed to realise it was merely time for recess.

"You look awful," Davey noted as he uneasily assessed the dark rings that had formed under her eyes.

"Davey, you can't say that!" objected Alice, then in agreement added, "You *do* look awful though, Ani."

"Sure, sure, pile on. I had to rush out this morning with no make-up," Analeigh answered defensively, despite never normally wearing any.

"Did you learn anything new?" asked Alice. Her jealousy over Analeigh's abilities had faded and she now found herself able to genuinely enjoy the daily magic shows that filled their break periods.

"Did you bring the doll?" Analeigh responded and flashed a quick grin.

Reaching into her backpack, Alice retrieved a small fashion doll and placed it on their schoolyard table, then hesitated. "Claire will be wanting this back," she reminded Analeigh, imagining having to face her six-year-old sister and explain that her friend had performed some form of disappearing act on one of her prized dolls.

Analeigh slowly nodded, then lifted her hand and gave her fingers a wriggle. The doll started to vibrate, before lifting off the table into a standing position. After a pause it stiffly began to march, while Analeigh's fingers twitched above as though she were puppeteering the doll with invisible strings.

"Creepy," assessed Davey.

"I think it's kind of festive! You know, like the *Nutcracker*?" replied Alice, mystified by the display.

"Festive? It's October. But I guess it kinda fits in with Halloween," he replied dryly.

"Maybe I'll go to Jackson's party as a witch this year," smiled Analeigh.

"If you do something like this while dressed as a witch," said Davey, pointing down at the small marching doll, "then the peasants and the townfolk are liable to form a torch-wielding mob," he warned, only half-joking.

Ignoring the negativity, Alice turned enthusiastically to Analeigh. "If Claire knew what you could do with her doll, she'd flip!"

Analeigh yawned, relaxed her hands and the doll fell flat and inanimate. "I don't want anyone to know about this, beyond you guys," she said seriously, then with forced levity added, "I'm kind of paranoid about getting caught and turned into some freak show or government experiment."

She yawned again and Alice's wonder for magic was quickly replaced with concern. "Did you sleep at all last night?" she asked, narrowing her eyes and once more staring at Analeigh's dark rings.

"School during the day, homework in the afternoon, magic at night." Analeigh shrugged in response.

"You said you'd take it slowly," Davey criticised.

"I am," answered Analeigh shortly.

"Maybe," he said hesitantly, "you should go... *slower*."

"Ryan's spirit was seen again Monday. It was in the morning paper. Every night he's in pain."

"That's not on you," he objected.

"If I *can* do something and *don't*, then it *becomes* on me," she answered, clearly annoyed.

It was rare that the friends fought, but since Ryan's death their arguments were becoming more frequent. Alice was not a fan of confrontation and immediately attempted to de-escalate the uncomfortable and recently all-too-familiar situation. "We're not saying you – we shouldn't do what we can..." she cooed motherly, "We're just saying you should think about your own health too. You've been doing too much, you haven't been sleeping, and you've got bags under your eyes."

"What final year student doesn't?!" Analeigh responded hotly, then began to laugh.

Alice and Davey shared a concerned glance, and Analeigh sighed. "Maybe you're right. I'm... clearly cranky," she conceded.

"So you'll take a break?" Alice ventured.

There was a long pause as Analeigh gave it serious consideration. "No," she finally answered, and her friends turned to her in surprise.

Davey went to say something but before he had the chance, Analeigh cut in. "Everything I come across in this book, I'm able to do. Sure, the technique can be hard and the movements are a struggle, but when I get it, I *really get it*! It's like second nature to me... If I keep practising for the next two nights – if I *can* get good enough by this Friday – I'd like to end this then." She stood and started to pace.

Alice and Davey looked at one another, but before they could respond, Analeigh quickly continued her ramblings, feeling sure that they might object.

"I can't... I can't stop while knowing that Ryan's out there, not when I feel that I'm so close. Not when every moment that I'm not trying to understand it, I'm racked with guilt about what I should be doing. If I do stop, then I won't be able to sleep anyway, knowing that the longer I wait, the more Ryan suffers. So really, if you let me try and get ready for Friday, then that's the quickest way to get me to have a good night's sleep again!" Having rambled out her argument she stopped, looked to her friends, and braced for their answer.

"Well... I don't know," Davey finally replied. With the book wholly in Analeigh's possession, he doubted that either he or Alice could do much to stop her, even if they did object. "How close are you *really* to being able to repair Ryan's spirit?"

Leaning uncomfortably close to his face, Analeigh began to twitch her right-hand thumb, index finger, and pointer rapidly together as though they were the pedi-palps of a spider, while Davey felt a strong and powerful itch on his left cheek, and Alice's jaw fell open in surprise. Reaching into her backpack, Alice retrieved and held out a small make-up mirror for Davey's inspection. He squinted and examined his face, running his finger across his smooth and unblemished cheek, where that morning the large dark scab cut by the raven had been.

He swore a shocked exclamation and Analeigh allowed a victorious grin. "I'm getting *really* close," she confirmed.

Friday, October 23rd. 11:55pm.

Davey looked out across the dark, moonlit road and sighed. There was half-eaten pizza sitting back in Alice's bedroom – probably once more being finished off by Claire – while *Bowery At Midnight* played on the small television without them. The room had been warm, and there had been snacks and soda and blankets, and the night was silent, cold and gloomy. His eyes settled on a dried floral wreath that marked the site of Ryan's crash and he longed for the abandoned coziness of Alice's room. The trio had once again snuck away from a perfectly good sleepover, down the stairs, out the door, into Davey's car and towards Hansen Road. They were parked again opposite the broken railing of the accident and sat staring at the section of road haunted by Ryan's spirit. Uneasily, Davey eyed the trees that surrounded them, wondering where the witch Bombalan might be right now, and then shook his head, deciding that he'd rather not know.

"Is anyone else suffering from a keen sense of déjà vu?" he asked, realising just how tired the weeks following Ryan's death had made him.

"This time it will be different," Analeigh promised.

"Again, I think we should have at least brought the pizza," he grumbled.

A greasy bag suddenly stuck out between Analeigh and Davey from the back seat and the waft of microwave popcorn followed.

"Orp-chorhn?" garbled Alice through a mouthful.

It had been freshly popped and was still warm, Analeigh having heated it up with pyrokinesis on their arrival. She had brought the unpopped kernels for the express purpose of showing off this newfound ability and Alice was suitably impressed.

Davey was not. "I'm... still not convinced eating that is safe," he answered, waving off the bag. "We don't know how Ani does... what she does, it could be some kind of radiation or something."

Alice shrugged and shovelled another handful into her mouth. "How do you think the microwave does it?" she laughed. "And besides—"

"He's here," Analeigh interrupted.

Across the road at the dropoff – roughly eleven metres away – the now-familiar sight of Ryan's semitransparent, torn, broken hands could be seen beginning their climb. They scraped and dragged themselves up and over the edge, but this time the trio were not content to simply sit, watch, and gape. Opening the passenger-side door and without a word, Analeigh exited the vehicle and walked into the centre of the road.

"Do you have to stand exactly there?!" Davey objected, remembering how they had witnessed a car speed through that very spot only two weeks earlier, but no response came from Analeigh as she stood rigid with intense concentration.

With a slight nod of nonverbal communication, Alice ran down the road a few metres, and Davey up, taking positions on opposite ends of the curve. They did so with plans to look out for cars, but both found it difficult to concentrate on keeping watch for danger as their eyes were inevitably drawn to the ghostly spectacle of their dead friend dragging himself across the road.

The spirit of Ryan Crosnor had just completed the twisted and jolting transition from its broken crawl to its disjointed walk when Analeigh started to sway. At first her movements were nothing more than a sapling caught in a breeze, but they grew and washed over her with fluidity and grace. She moved slowly, with deliberate purpose and exactness, and looked almost as though she were performing tai chi.

The spirit of Ryan Crosnor paid these movements no heed, and continued to drag and stumble its feet towards her.

Analeigh danced and the graceful movements became more shuddery as she snapped and popped her joints and limbs from one extreme to another, while the ghost groaned and moaned, and she continued her dance.

With less than five metres between them, the Moon was stolen by clouds and the four figures were shrouded in darkness, but only Alice and Davey would remain as such.

The distance was two metres, and Davey's heart raced at how close the ghastly figure had drawn towards his friend, and Analeigh began to glow.

At first it was a vague luminescence – like a glow-in-the-dark sticker that had not received enough light – but quickly she brightened with white flames that licked skyward. Soon she was engulfed in a blinding halo of fire and she continued to dance with movements that jumped from wavy to erratic and were as unpredictable as the flames that had swallowed her.

And the distance had closed to nothingness.

Reaching out from the void, a dark, broken hand – visible only in silhouette – touched Analeigh, and Ryan's semitransparent feet, torn and broken, lifted off from the black road. Ryan floated, suspended in mid-air as if held by countless threads from above, and Analeigh danced her mad dance with fevered speed and movement while white-hot ribbons of light snaked from her body and connected with Ryan's head, chest, and stomach. From where the beams connected, the fire spread and the ghost of Ryan Crosnor took on a dull glow that slowly intensified.

The light expanded and spread across Ryan's body as broken bones and twisted limbs began to snap back into position, then heal over with torn flesh made whole, while Analeigh dimmed but did not go out. Soon Ryan was as a blinding ball of lightning that lit the surrounding road and forest with daylight, while Analeigh dulled to noon, then faded into midnight. Slowly Ryan descended back down onto the bitumen – spirit body fully repaired – and stood opposite Analeigh, who swayed, but no longer in dance.

"Thank you," Ryan mouthed wordlessly, then dissipated into sparks like fireflies that floated and faded away.

And Analeigh fainted.

Saturday, October 24th. 12:10am.

Alice took the legs and Davey the arms. It required the two friends' combined strength to carry Analeigh's limp and unconscious body from the middle of the road, and Davey did his best to drive the words 'dead weight' from his mind. They hefted her into the car, placed her upright in the back seat and buckled her in. The worn tyres screeched as Davey turned the car downhill and continued to do so with each corner taken too fast. Much like the night Ryan had died, caution was forgotten and safety replaced by haste. Davey drove and Alice asked whether they should be going straight to the hospital or to Analeigh's house to wake her parents, while his mind raced as fast as the car, unable to move past what had happened and what could be done.

He had **told** her that she should be more careful. He had cautioned her on how they had no idea what forces she was messing with, or what kind of energy she was utilising. And now he struggled to force his thoughts away from accounts of nuclear meltdowns. He tried not to think of the term 'acute radiation poisoning' or how it would cause her hair and nails to fall out and her eyes to bleed. He tried not to think about how it was almost always fatal or how close he and Alice had been to her and whether or not they themselves had been exposed.

The hospital or Analeigh's? Davey! Are we going to the hospital or to Analeigh's?

He could vaguely hear Alice asking the question and found that he had no answer. Regardless of whether they chose to go to the hospital or to Analeigh's parents', Davey wasn't sure that either would be able to help her, and he really wasn't sure what they would say they had been doing, or what they had done. Alice was breathing heavily and he was driving erratically, and some part of Davey's subconscious noted that they were probably both having panic attacks.

The car bounced down onto the flats from the last of Hansen Road and fishtailed its way into what is laughably known as Clarke Valley's main street, and with an intersection coming up, Davey's mind thundered while Alice's words continued to echo in his head – or possibly were still being repeated: "Analeigh's or the hospital?" – then, without warning, Analeigh opened her eyes and softly asked, "Did it work?"

The car slowed, the panic subsided, and Davey's pulse still raced.

It had worked.

Though none of them knew it at the time, the ghost of Ryan Crosnor would never again be sighted by the people of Clarke Valley, and tomorrow night, for the first time in five long weeks, the dark twists and tight turns of Hansen Road would rest undisturbed.

Saturday, October 24th. 4:00pm.

It had been a long and emotional night, and it hadn't ended with the ghost. Following the restoration of Ryan's spirit and her brief unconsciousness, Analeigh had said that she felt woozy and wanted to go home rather than return to the sleepover. Instead they had gone back to Alice's bedroom and argued. Neither Alice nor Davey thought that she was in any condition to be left by herself – let alone be allowed to drive. They had argued that she should be checked over by a doctor, but Analeigh had refused to be taken to the hospital or to have any adults brought into the matter whatsoever. She was relentless in her insistence and eventually they compromised.

It was agreed that they would not take her to the hospital and that no one would be told she had fainted, provided that she committed to resting for the remainder of the weekend. It was further agreed that she would spend the rest of said weekend within the confines of her house and that she would lay off the use of magic for a long while, if not permanently. Analeigh had feigned annoyance at this proposal, but agreed. Secretly she felt more than woozy. She felt exhausted, dreadfully nauseous, and strangely morose. Deep down, she doubted that she would have had the energy to go out over the next two days, or to perform magic ever again, regardless of her friends' insistence.

Once the agreement had been shook on, they took two cars over to Analeigh's house – Davey driving his own and

Alice driving Analeigh's with her as passenger. Because of Analeigh's exhaustion, they had needed to help her in through the door, and up to her room. Once they had gotten her into bed, they reconfirmed her agreement to stay in all weekend and Alice warned that she would be calling to check up on her, then the pair left for Alice's in Davey's car. After dropping Alice home, Davey continued on to his own house, the sleepover having officially ended prematurely.

It wasn't until 2am that this had all been sorted and Alice was finally able to lie down. She dozed – drifting through near-sleep – until 4pm, when she sat up, yawned, and wandered downstairs. Despite having spent most of the day in bed, she still felt exhausted and vaguely wondered whether Davey had gotten up in time for work. She doubted that he had.

Approaching the home phone mounted to the wall in the kitchen, Alice rotated the dial to enter in Analeigh's phone number. Placing the receiver to her ear, she leaned against the wall, and listened. The dial tone rang, followed by the soft muffled clatter of the phone on the other end being retrieved from its cradle.

"Harris residence," came a clipped voice.

Alice found the normalcy of the answer reassuring after the strangeness of the night before. "It's Alice, Missus Harris, is Analeigh there?"

"Oh, Alice dear!" said Mrs Harris enthusiastically, "I hope you're feeling okay. Analeigh tells me she had to leave your place early last night – I hope it isn't the flu! She's been in bed all day, but I can wake her if you'd like?"

Alice smiled, gladdened that Analeigh had kept to her side of the late-night promise. "No, it's okay, Missus Harris, don't worry about it. Tell her I'll talk to her on Monday and to get well soon," she answered with a yawn.

"I'll let her sleep then," said Mrs Harris, all but beaming through the phone at one of her daughter's oldest friends.

"Yes, do!" agreed Alice with equal warmth, then paused, second-guessing whether or not she should inform Analeigh's mum that her daughter had fainted. She turned the thought over in her mind and then, reasoning that if Analeigh kept to her side of the bargain, she would not likely faint again, decided against it.

Provided that she does keep to her side of the bargain, Alice thought, and frowned. "Oh and Missus Harris?"

"Yes, dear?"

"If you see her up and about, please warn – I mean, *tell* Analeigh I'll be checking in on her tomorrow."

"You're such a dear," she praised, before farewelling her caller, and hanging up.

Aren't I just? thought Alice smugly, then yawned and made breakfast for dinner.

On Monday, school came and went, and Alice grew concerned. She and Analeigh share two afternoon lessons on a Monday, and Analeigh had been a no-show in both. Neither had she made an appearance in the class that she usually shared with Davey, nor did she meet them during morning recess or afternoon break.

Alice and Davey had talked worriedly at lunchtime in regards to their Friday night activity and how much of a drain it appeared to have had on Analeigh. She had already seemed off over the last week, becoming cross and argumentative with them in the days preceding the latest incident on Hansen Road, and that was before the exertion of the night had caused her to faint. Alice was concerned that the stress of the night and the pressure leading up to it had damaged Analeigh's psyche. She worried that Analeigh had pushed herself too far and that the emotional and physical drain over the weeks since Ryan's death had caused her serious illness – some form of extreme emotional exhaustion, perhaps. Davey's concerns were less psychological and more physical in nature. Echoing his popcorn comments from three nights prior, he pondered once more exactly what kind of energy it was that had surged through his friend to allow her to do what she had been doing. Fearing exposure himself, he had continually checked his own pupils and skin for signs of change in the days since.

When the last lesson let out, Alice made for student parking relieved that the day was finally over. She had been so concerned with Analeigh's absence that she had failed to concentrate on anything else and dully realised that she had likely flunked a test worth 30% of her grade. She sped home five over the speed limit – only slowing as she passed Ryan's fatal curve – and on arrival all but sprinted to the kitchen phone to dial in Analeigh's number.

Mrs Harris answered and, after a brief exchange of pleasantries, the receiver was handed to Analeigh.

"Alice," she said flatly.

"Ani, are you okay?" asked Alice.

"Of course, why do you ask?" came the slow response.

Alice paused to ponder the question. At first she was annoyed Analeigh had asked it when the reasons for her concern were so obvious, then she felt worried by how sincerely Analeigh had sounded while doing so. "Well, you weren't in school today, you see?" she finally responded.

"Ah," said Analeigh. "I'll be there tomorrow."

"Tomorrow," repeated Alice.

"Tomorrow," confirmed Analeigh who, with no further comment hung up the phone, leaving Alice with nothing more than a dead tone and a feeling of unease to indicate that the conversation had ended.

Placing the phone back onto the cradle, she felt a wave of confusion and concern wash over her. Joining this unease was something new. There was, somewhere mixed in amongst her emotions – barely felt, but growing – a dull hum of fear. It was a nagging fear that at first seemed subtle and distant, yet grew over the following minutes and hours, and by the time Monday had given way to Tuesday, sat prominently in her consciousness.

On Tuesday, Analeigh had again made no effort to come to school, and after classes ended for the day Alice had tried contacting her once more. The call was answered by Mrs Harris, who informed her that Analeigh had gone out, and expressed surprise that it was not with Alice or Davey she had done so. This, along with Analeigh's strange distant nature during their call on Monday, concerned Alice greatly. When Wednesday morning came and Analeigh's beat-up old Ford finally made an appearance in the school parking lot, Alice felt her breath catch and her heart race. She was annoyed that she had been lied to when Analeigh had said she would be in school Tuesday, and she was concerned about where – when Alice had called last night – she had otherwise been. It was, however, beyond anything else, a feeling of immense relief she felt when the rusted driver-side door of the vehicle opened and the girl who stepped out wore a wide, cheerful smile that gave no clue to recent traumas. The dark rings under her eyes were still prominent and her cheeks did not seem so rosy as they had been even just a few days earlier, but there was a spring in her step.

With warmth and energy in her voice, she called out, "Alice, Davey, hey!" and greeted each of them with a tight hug.

"Feeling better?" asked Alice.

"I'll say!" said Analeigh, "I slept like a baby last night."

Before Alice could press for an explanation of Analeigh's absence, a teacher's voice from the class-rooms yelled at them to get moving and they were forced to go their separate ways for the next several hours. On Wednesdays the only class the trio share is English Studies, which takes place just before recess and in which their exhaustingly monotone teacher, Mr Bowden, immediately began to drone on in great depths about the significance of red curtains in the class's group study text.

"They are red, symbolising vitality and passion – of course of a sexual nature – but they are also tattered, suggesting said passion is unfulfilled," he recited, directly from a weathered-looking teacher's guide.

From the front of the classroom (where he had been moved to due to his constant disturbances) Cole muttered, "Ask Drizzle about unfulfilled passion," just loud enough for the whole classroom to hear, while the teacher – either unaware or unwilling to respond – droned on.

"And of course, the author takes the time to describe the wooden curtain rod, which is not only notably phallic, but is also snapped, indicating some level of impotence."

"Drizzle knows all about things that are notably phallic – impotent too, I'd bet." Cole loudly whispered his continued contribution to the classroom discussion and Davey ground his teeth.

Leaning over to Davey, who was one desk to her right, Alice whispered, "Forget him, if there's anything here that's notably phallic, it's Cole," which caused Davey to unclench his jaw into a smile and a few nearby classmates to laugh.

"I'll say it's notable, probably my best feature!" agreed Cole, unwilling to let well enough alone, and the teacher sighed heavily, remembering that he had once dreamt of writing great adventure novels before he had become a teacher. "Do you have anything to add, Mister Sheridan?" Mr Bowden asked tiredly, rubbing his fingers over his eyes.

"Yes, sir, Mister Bee!" began Cole cockily, before standing up straight at attention. As he stood rigid and unmoving, the chatter in the classroom fell silent.

"Mister Sheridan?" said the teacher after a confused pause.

Without responding, Cole punched himself in the face, the blow knocking him backwards into the desk behind him. Limply he flopped to the floor and the classroom erupted in a hysteria of humour and confusion, while the teacher babbled in shock at something in his twenty years of teaching he had never before seen and only Alice, who sat to the right of Analeigh, noticed or appreciated the significance of the small hand movements her friend was performing under the desk. Analeigh was twisting her fingers in the same way that she had done when moving Claire's doll and as Cole sat up and wobbled slightly, Alice elbowed Davey, drawing his attention to Analeigh's actions.

Leaning across Alice's desk, he whispered, "I think you gave him a concussion," not the least bit displeased at the prospect, and Analeigh smiled and continued to twist, jerk, and pop her fingers in unnatural movements that quickly cycled from fluid to jarring.

Davey remained leaning over Alice's desk and watching, mesmerised as Analeigh's fingers wriggled and twitched in ways that seemingly defied the restraints of muscle, bone, and ligament. Her actions held his attention like a hypnotic spell that broke only when his fellow students erupted into screams, and Alice whispered, "Oh my god." into his ear.

Returning his attention to the front of the classroom, Davey saw that Cole was now backed into the corner of the room with his spine pressed flat against the blackboard, one arm outstretched. Between two fingers he held out a small white-and-red rock and Davey squinted in confusion, trying to make out what it could be. Then Cole's hand dramatically twisted and dropped the object to the floor and a girl in the front row vomited, and a boy fainted.

Davey stared at the dropped item, his mind unable to place it, then with an erratic jerk Cole brought his arm up towards his own face and plunged his hand into his mouth. His fingers tightened, spasmed, twisted, and then retreated, holding yet another blood-covered white pebble between two of his rigid digits. Blood flowed from his mouth and down over his chin, and he dropped this second pearl to the floor, only to plunge his hand back in for a third.

"Oh my god." agreed Davey, his face having gone pale white.

The third tooth came out and was quickly discarded and, as Cole thrust his hand in for another extraction, the teacher regained his composure and attempted to restrain him. He fought to wrestle Cole's arms down away from his face, trying to pin them by his side, and Alice began to shake Analeigh, desperate to break her concentration and cease her brutal actions. Cole struggled as Mr Bowden pulled him to the floor and pinned him, and while to anyone else within the classroom it would have appeared as though this was the intervention that ended Cole's truly insane behaviour, Davey knew otherwise.

He had seen how, while everyone else's attention was drawn to Cole and the teacher, Alice had shook Analeigh and harshly whisper for her to stop.

He had seen Cole break free an arm, and plunge it towards his face once more, and grab hold of yet another tooth.

And he had seen how Cole's attempts at self-mutilation had only halted when Alice delivered a hard, stinging slap across the side of Analeigh's face.

Cole was dragged to the nurse's office, a doctor was called, class was dismissed, and Analeigh marched directly towards the student carpark with Alice and Davey following closely behind.

"Are you insane?" Alice demanded.

"He was being a jerk. He was a jerk to Ryan and now he's being a jerk to Davey. He got what he deserved," Analeigh answered coolly.

Davey gave no response, still stunned into silence over what he had just witnessed and how his friend could have been responsible for such brutality.

"Yeah, he's a dick, doesn't mean you can freaking mutilate him!" hissed Alice in response.

Analeigh opened her car door and sat down within. "Technically, he mutilated himself," she answered and closed the door on her friends.

"Where are you going?!" squealed Alice in frustration.

Giving no answer, Analeigh started the engine and drove away.

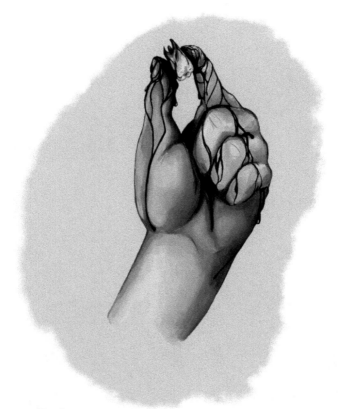

"His fingers tightened, spasmed, twisted, and then retreated, holding yet another blood-covered white pebble between two of his rigid digits."

Part 4: The Wraith

Friday, October 30th. 1:00pm.

It had been a week since Analeigh repaired and freed the spirit of Ryan Crosnor from Hansen Road, and talk of the ghost had dramatically fallen off. With no more reports of sightings since the *Gazette* article on the 21st, people had begun to move on. Chatter around the school-yard was now more focused on recent and upcoming events, with students either excitedly talking about their Halloween plans, now only a day away, or whispering about the Year 12 student who tore out his own teeth.

Since Wednesday, no conversation between Alice and Davey had lasted much longer than a few sentences before reverting back to the subject of Analeigh. She had not yet returned to school following the much-talk-ed-about incident and neither Alice nor Davey were surprised. The brutality of what Analeigh had done to Cole was something that the two were still trying to come to terms with. While Alice was certain they would eventu-ally work through the divide it had created, she was also somewhat ashamedly gladdened by Analeigh's absence. She wanted to give Analeigh the benefit of the doubt and felt sure that in time things would go back to normal between them. But for now, whenever she thought of her friend, she couldn't help but envision Cole tearing apart his own face, and thinking how it was Analeigh who had been responsible.

When lunch came, Alice and Davey sat down, exchanged pleasantries, and fell quiet. An awkward silence dragged, then Davey again resurfaced the topic.

"Cole has always been a jackass, but even so..." He let the thought trail off. "The punch was warranted, a long time coming even... but the teeth," he shuddered. "The teeth were twisted."

"I *slapped* her, I can't believe I slapped Analeigh," whispered Alice as she turned an apple over in her hand, finding that she had no appetite for it. "I don't even like arguing with her and now I've – I've *struck* her!" She threw the apple idly into a nearby bush.

They sat in silence, not looking at one another, while the noise of the schoolyard continued around them.

"You had to," responded Davey long after Alice's comment had died away.

"Had to what?" she asked, having forgotten what she'd said.

"Slap her. You had to slap her," he said distantly.

"Oh," she answered. Much of their conversation was repeats of what they had already discussed over the last few days, several times over. "Cole didn't come to school today, or yesterday."

"No. He's probably had to go to an emergency dentistry appointment, or psychology appointment, or he's just plain scared shitless," Davey suggested.

Alice nodded slowly. "Yeah, there's that," she agreed.

"I'm a little... concerned myself," he admitted.

"About Analeigh?"

"About what she did, and how she did it," he replied, putting away his unfinished, unstarted lunch with an equal lack of appetite.

"Yeah..." agreed Alice reluctantly. "It's been a tough month." She said, repeating the reassurance she'd been unsuccessfully giving herself.

"We've all had a tough month, but you and I aren't going around making people mutilate themselves," he replied in a near-inaudible whisper.

Alice stood and began to pace contemplatively, while Davey's head tracked her movements back and forth as though she were the ball in a tennis match.

She paused her pacing. "You remember that doll I used to have?"

He furrowed his brow in confusion. "The red-headed porcelain one that you used to bring everywhere?"

Alice nodded. "I never told you what happened to it."

Confused by the abrupt change in topic, Davey scratched his head thoughtfully. She hadn't had that doll for years and he hadn't thought about it for just as long. "No, you never told me," he agreed, shaking his head. "I just assumed that you had lost it, or grew out of it."

She began to pace again. "No, not lost. Destroyed."

He sat up straight with a surprised jolt. "Destroyed?"

"Yeah, by me."

"But why?"

"I don't know – I didn't mean to, or I *did*, but hadn't meant to mean to," she rambled.

Davey took a swig of his water bottle and cocked his head, waiting for elaboration.

"It was just after my mother died – I was eleven, remember?" She paused and took a deep breath. "I had learned about the accident and gone to my room, and I was just sort of standing there and not thinking or maybe thinking too much, and the doll was a gift from my mum, and I just smashed it."

Davey said nothing, turning over what he had heard in his mind. He had never known Alice to suffer fits of anger or destruction and could tell from the tears in her eyes that, though this had taken place roughly five years ago, it was still a very fresh wound. He wondered whether she had told anyone about it before and then realised that she was waiting for some form of response.

"Because it was a gift from your mum? It reminded you too much of her?" he ventured.

She laughed and a sob escaped her throat, "See, that's just it, I don't know! I was just feeling so *much*, it was anger and sadness and confusion, and there was just so much that without thinking – animalistically – I lashed out... I don't even know if I realised I was doing it or what I was doing it to until it was done, and then my doll was smashed and my mum was still dead."

He took her hand and gave it a light squeeze. "And you think Cole was maybe just... Analeigh's porcelain doll?" he asked, uneasy with the euphemism.

Alice let out a shaky sigh. "I hope so."

"You only broke one doll, right?" he questioned, only slightly joking. "If she makes a habit of it, if she *breaks more toys...*" he continued hesitantly.

"I know," agreed Alice. "I think she just might need us now and I'm really trying to let myself be there for her."

"Well, I'm here too if she does need us," affirmed Davey and she squeezed his hand back in thanks and acknowledgement. He paused and thought about the last time they had seen Analeigh and how her car had sped away from them, off down Hansen Road. He doubted that she would be coming to their weekly sleepover tonight. "Have you spoken to her since Wednesday?"

"Not yet. I think it was a good idea to give her some time to cool off – for us all to cool off – but I'll stop by hers after school and make sure she's okay and still on for tomorrow," she replied, letting go of Davey's hand and wiping away a tear with the back of her own.

"Do you want me to come?" he asked, trying to be supportive but hoping that Alice would answer in the negative.

"No, that's okay. I don't want it to look like an intervention."

Quietly Davey wondered if an intervention wasn't such a bad idea and then, realising what Alice had said, snapped out of his contemplation. "On for tomorrow? But today is Friday, don't you mean *on for tonight*?"

"No, tomorrow is Halloween so we're not doing a sleepover tonight. We discussed it back in September, remember?"

They had made their plans for Halloween only a day before Ryan's crash and Alice was not surprised that Davey had lost track of time or forgotten what they had decided to do in all that had happened since.

"Oh," he answered, dramatically slapping a hand to his forehead. "That's fallen on the thirty-first this year?" he said sarcastically.

"Every year!" she mocked playfully. "Weren't you curious about all the carved pumpkins or the candy in all the stores!" she continued, relieved by the more light-hearted change of topic.

"Speaking of candy, I assume we're still trick or treating with your sister?" he asked.

"And then to Jackson's party," Alice confirmed with a nod. "You *do* have a costume, right?"

"Of course!" he promised.

"The pirate costume?"

"Yarh," he admitted and Alice smiled.

"How many times is that?"

"Three years running. I've got to get my money's worth out of that eye patch, you know?"

She laughed, and the school bell rang signifying that lunch had come to an end and the two began to walk their separate ways.

"My place, tomorrow at three!" she shouted.

"Yarrhhh," he replied again and then, dropping the act, added in a more serious tone, "Good luck with Analeigh... be careful."

Friday, October 30th. 3:45pm.

Alice walked past the plastic skeletons and foam-cut gravestones that decorated Analeigh's lawn, up the porch steps, and towards the door, which swung outwards before she had even had the chance to knock. In the doorway stood Analeigh, who squinted into the light.

"Oh, Analeigh!" Alice started, surprised. She had rehearsed what she was going to say many times over the last two days, but now her mind had gone blank. It was the sight of Analeigh that had derailed her train of thought; her friend looked haggard. Her eyes were bloodshot and the bags under them were darker and larger than Alice had ever before seen – on any person.

"Alice," Analeigh finally said, blinking slowly. "Sorry I wasn't in school today, I think what I did yesterday took a lot out of me... both emotionally and... *otherwise.*"

Alice considered pointing out that the horrible incident with Cole had been two days ago – not yesterday – but then considered the possibility that Analeigh might have done something else since. Not wishing to learn of any further horrible actions, she decided to let the mistake go. Placing one hand on Analeigh's wrist and, suppressing a recoil of shock at how cold her skin was to the touch, she simply asked if she were okay.

"Yes... no," Analeigh admitted. "I don't know what came over me, it's like every angry thought I'd ever felt boiled to the surface all at once..."

162

"You're... feeling alright now, though?" Alice asked, not sure how to word what she really wanted to know.

"I don't feel anger any more, just regret and embarrassment." said Analeigh, forcing a smile that came out as a grimace. "How's Cole doing?"

"No one's heard," admitted Alice, "but he plays football, so he would have lost those teeth eventually anyway," she added, attempting some levity.

Analeigh did not laugh, but pulled that same failed smile. Neither spoke and the moment grew awkward.

"Will you be coming to mine tomorrow?" Alice clumsily asked, rushing to break the silence.

"For trick or treating? Yes, of course," confirmed Analeigh, speaking slowly as if she were in a trance.

"Great," said Alice. "Three o'clock."

"Three o'clock," echoed Analeigh.

Unsure what else she could say, Alice slowly turned to leave, took two steps down the porch and then turned back. "Oh and Ani?"

"Alice?"

"I'm sorry I slapped you."

"Oh?" Analeigh placed a hand to the side of her face. "I'm glad that you did," she muttered gravely.

Saturday, October 31st. Halloween. 3:10pm.

Alice, Davey, and Claire stood waiting in the front yard of Alice's home. Claire – refusing to allow herself to be called cute – had done herself up as some sort of goblin, and Alice – who had no such objection to being called cute – had donned a pair of cat-ears and a tail, while Davey was fiddling with a leather eyepatch that sported a white Jolly Roger.

Analeigh was nowhere to be seen.

"It's past three," moaned Claire impatiently, looking in through the kitchen window at the wall clock.

"We'll give her five more minutes and then we'll go," promised Alice, shooting an uncertain sideways glance towards Davey.

Analeigh had never been known for punctuality and was running only ten minutes late yet, despite this, Davey and Alice were already feeling slightly nervous.

"All the best candy will be gone!" Claire objected, all but bouncing in place.

Alice shot another look at Davey, hoping for support, and he met her eyes.

"She's right, the good candy always goes first." He shrugged and Alice's look turned dirty.

"Fine," she sighed. "I'll just call her to make sure she's on the way."

Davey watched through the window as Alice walked back into the house, dialled the phone, then spoke with furrowed brow. The conversation was short and within a minute she had hung up and was walking back outside looking confused.

"Can we go now?" demanded Claire.

"Her mum says she left half an hour ago. She should've been here by now," answered Alice, ignoring Claire's hand as it tugged at the back of her cat-suit.

"It's... probably nothing," said Davey with forced false positivity. Alice shot him an unconvinced look and he added, "She's probably just left everything to the last minute and is digging through bargain bins trying to piece together a costume."

"Maybe..." Alice allowed.

"Aliiiiiice," whined Claire, before dramatically flopping onto her back in the grass.

"You two go up and down the street and start trick or treating. I'll wait here and if Analeigh hasn't arrived by the time you're back, we'll move on to the next street without her," offered Davey.

"I want Davey to take me!" shouted Claire, grabbing his hand.

Alice laughed. "Okay, your plan but with me waiting here instead?"

"Done," he agreed.

"Done!" parroted Claire.

Retrieving a cola from the fridge and sitting down on the steps, Alice nervously eyed the costumed children already making their way up and down the street. Her father worked late shifts (this was why she was expected to chaperone her sister's Halloween each year) and because no one was going to be home, they had intended to leave the house lights off to show trick-or-treaters that no candy could be found there, and now she was sitting on the front porch. "I'm going to cop a lot of abuse for being here with no candy, you know?" she mumbled to Davey.

"We'll be back soon," he promised, then, turning to Claire, added, "Let's go, munchkin."

"I'm a goblin," she corrected, and the two wandered off towards the next-door neighbour's house.

Alice continued to sit with her cola, taking sips and disappointing trick-or-treaters, until half an hour had passed and Claire and Davey returned, having completed the full street circuit. The neighbourhood was now full of witches, ghosts, and gargoyles of all forms – all comically short – and all carrying absurdly large bags of junk food.

"It's a good thing you have a little sister, Alice," said Davey, shoveling a handful of chocolate nuts into his mouth. "Trick or treating stockpiles my candy supplies for the whole year."

"I'm not sure chaperones are supposed to get candy," laughed Alice.

"Shh, don't say that too loudly, people might catch on." he whispered dramatically, then, in a more serious tone, asked, "No word from Analeigh?"

Alice shook her head slowly. "Not a peep."

As the afternoon wore on, Alice and Davey continued to take Claire door to door collecting treats. While they walked, they held out silent hope that any masked figure who walked towards them might be their friend – moving to catch up – but as the Sun set and the houses turned off their porch lights, it became abundantly clear that Analeigh would not be joining them.

With their treat bags full, Alice and Davey walked Claire home and joined her in eating some candy as they waited for Alice's father to return from work. Once he arrived, they deposited what little they hadn't yet eaten in Alice's room, then, leaving Claire behind, departed for Jackson's Halloween party.

Saturday, October 31st. Halloween. 9:30pm.

Being that Jackson's house was just two streets over from Alice's, the plan was to head there on foot, enjoy the festivities, and then walk – or likely stumble – their way back to Alice's to crash for the night. Doing so had become somewhat of a tradition over the last few years, as Jackson had thrown a Halloween party annually since they were thirteen. Back then it was party games and an early night, but as they had matured, so too had the festivities. It was where the friends had formed many of their best memories – where Ryan had had his first kiss, and Analeigh her first taste of alcohol – and if you were to have told either Alice or Davey a month and a half ago that they would be walking to Jackson's Halloween party without them, neither would have believed it.

"I'm sure she's fine," Davey stated unprompted.

"Sure?" asked Alice.

"Hopeful." he amended.

Alice sighed heavily. "I'm sure she is," she agreed. "She looked pretty tired yesterday, so maybe she got halfway to my house and realised she just didn't have the party spirit."

"Maybe," agreed Davey, not allowing himself to question why, if that were the case, she had not found the time or courtesy to call them.

They reached the driveway of Jackson's house and could hear loud music and louder partying going on within. A skeleton was sat by the front door with an empty candy bowl in its lap and a lanyard around its neck instructing guests to follow the garden path down the side of the house in order to join the festivities.

"Ready?" asked Davey.

"Ready," nodded Alice and they opened the side-gate and made their way towards the backyard and its increasingly noisy sounds.

At least half of their year level was there and the boisterous revelry was amplified by an almost certainly spiked punchbowl. There was dancing, and laughing, and kissing, and singing out of key, and Alice and Davey found a quiet corner in the kitchen and poured a drink. Suddenly the bathroom door flew open and Jackson stumbled out, down the hallway and into the kitchen, dressed as a spaceman and struggling with his fly.

"Some party!" he called with a goofy smile.

"Some party," agreed Davey.

"Glad you guys came. If you need to crash, you can – plenty of floor space – and my parents are gone until Monday." He pulled a bag of chips from the pantry and threw it to Melvin, who was waving an empty bowl in the doorway with one hand and half-hanging off of Helen with the other.

"Thanks, Jackson," answered Alice, not bothering to remind him how close she lived.

"What's with Analeigh?" Jackson mumbled, pouring himself an overly strong vodka and soda. He took a sip and winced, then added, "I thought she'd be coming with you guys..."

"Sorry Analeigh couldn't make it, she's feeling... off," Alice answered – it wasn't a lie.

"Huh?" he responded with obvious confusion. "Analeigh's been here for hours, she showed up with that jackass Cole, who by the way," he gesticulated, "was *not* invited."

"What?!" demanded Alice, confused and angry.

"Yeah, they're somewhere together, they've been hanging off each other all night. His face is all kinds of messed up," Jackson burped.

"Oh," said Alice.

"Oh," said Davey.

They shared a worried look and Alice felt concern and fury once more boil to the surface. She had been doing her best to give her friend the benefit of the doubt – perhaps against her own better judgement – but this felt like a step too far. There were things that were done in the heat of the moment, and then there was cruelty. To lash out in anger was one thing, but to knowingly ditch your friends – without so much as a word – despite knowing that this would worry them was another.

And why Cole? Analeigh likes Cole even less than most people do – her actions the other day made that abundantly clear – so why would Analeigh have come to the party with Cole, of all people? her mind uncomfortably questioned.

Alice wasn't sure what Analeigh was up to, or why she would be off with someone who only days earlier she had caused such physical damage – but whatever it was, it couldn't be good. She tried to convince herself that Analeigh wasn't planning to cause him any further harm. That she had maybe met up with Cole just to check on him, and that she wasn't playing some kind of sick game. But any attempted self-assurance fell short. As much as she loved her friend and despite how long they had known each other, the last week had caused doubt to creep into her mind. As she and Davey left the conversation and began to search the house, she found that she did so not out of concern for Analeigh's wellbeing, but out of concern for Cole's, and what Analeigh may be doing to him.

They checked the garden, and the shed, and the living room, and any small nook or cranny that lay in between, and though they found plenty of classmates stealing away some privacy in order to share a moment, they did not find Analeigh.

"Maybe Jackson is wrong. I'm pretty sure he was loaded," Davey optimistically suggested while they walked down the hallway and checked every door on their way to Jackson's bedroom.

Alice doubted that Jackson was wrong, but gave no response. She was too angry and too worried to speak.

The door to Jackson's bedroom was closed but again, before Alice had even had the chance to knock – not that she was sure she had intended to – it flew open and on the other side stood Analeigh. She looked as though she were a typical witch, not unlike the many others they had seen that night as costumes and on countless decorations. She was dressed in black socks with a short, tight black dress and matching lipstick. Her skin was grey and Alice wondered if it was naturally like that or from make-up, and found herself certain that it was the former. To complete the look she wore a tall pointed black hat.

"Alice," she simply said.

"What the hell?!" Alice spat.

"What." said Analeigh.

"We were supposed to take Claire trick or treating!"

"Come on, Alice. I just didn't want to miss half of the biggest party of the year to go trick or treating with some ten-year-old," Analeigh answered coolly.

"She's six!" Alice cried.

"There's no need to yell," Analeigh responded with infuriating calm.

"We waited for you! I sat outside for half an hour! We were worried and you didn't even call!"

Behind Analeigh appeared Cole, who was dressed as a boxer complete with inflatable gloves, satin shorts, and a bare chest covered in black lipstick. He smiled listlessly, revealing the many missing teeth that complemented his costume's authenticity. "Why's all the shouting?" he slurred.

"You're with him, after what you did?" hissed Alice, revulsion now replacing her fury.

"That's disgusting," muttered Davey, feeling faint and ill.

"Disgusting?" repeated Cole, unaware of Analeigh's role in his mutilation and not understanding the full context of the conversation. "You're no prize yerself, Drizzle," he drunkenly belly-laughed.

Usually this would be the cue for Davey to give back an insult in kind, but he now found that he had nothing but sympathy for Cole, along with fear at how unhinged their friend had evidently become. He shot a glance at Alice and she – taking a deep breath to calm herself – nodded, and reached out a hand for Analeigh's arm.

"I think we should leave, Ani," she said softly, desperately trying to de-escalate the situation and appeal to her friend's better judgement.

"Maybe you two should go," agreed Analeigh, shaking Alice's hand free from her arm. She leaned towards Cole and wrapped her now-free arm around his. "Besides, maybe it's good you two saw this. I know you both have a thing for me." She winked at Alice. "But maybe now you can move on and settle for each other."

The accusation both startled and embarrassed Davey. His mouth gaped and he was equal parts speechless and paralysed by his long-time friend's sudden and uncharacteristic cruelty.

Alice was not. Moving fast, she threw the hand that she had extended only moments earlier in friendship as a hard slap towards Analeigh's face, but found it caught and held by an invisible force mere centimetres from connection.

"Never again," whispered Analeigh, and Alice felt her hand released and allowed it to fall down to her side.

"Ani – " she pleaded.

"We're done," came the steely response. Analeigh turned and went back into the bedroom with Cole and, without anyone having touched the door, it slammed in Davey's and Alice's faces.

They left the party and Alice spattered profanity in anger and annoyance. "Grief is one thing, being angry is one thing – but that was active cruelty! She was trying to be a bitch!" she vented.

"I think," Davey began, "we have to consider that her magic has caused something to go wrong."

"*You think*!" she spat rhetorically. "But how can floating marbles and moving objects cause something like that! It's like she isn't even Analeigh any more!"

He stopped dead. "Maybe she isn't," he pondered. "And maybe *her* magic isn't what's responsible."

"*Mother Bombalan*?!" Alice cried, shocked by the suggestion.

"Analeigh did steal her book." He nodded gravely. "Maybe Bombalan took it personally."

"But what about the charms?" she asked, ringing her bracelet in his face.

"They're Mother Bombalan's charms. She probably made them and knows how to get around them."

"And she, what – *cursed her*?" Alice asked, turning pale.

"Cursed, hexed, possessed," suggested Davey, running his mind over the various texts he had read not two weeks earlier. "I don't really know," he admitted, "but as you said – what we saw back there, that wasn't how our friend acts. She has never acted like that. And I don't care how angry, or tired, or grief-stricken Analeigh is, that wasn't her."

Alice nodded and began walking again, feeling hopeful at the prospect that her friend wasn't entirely lost, guilty for almost having given up on her, and concerned about what could be done to remedy it. "So what do we do?"

Davey fell in step beside her. "We go to Analeigh's house, tonight, and we get the book back. Tomorrow we visit Mother Bombalan – during the day – and ask her to forgive Analeigh and to lift the curse," he outlined simply.

"Do you think that will work?"

"What other choice do we have?" he answered, honestly wondering, and the two friends finished the remainder of the walk back to Alice's house in silence.

Saturday, October 31st. Halloween. 11:00pm.

Mrs Harris hadn't thought it strange when Alice and Davey arrived without her daughter. The three of them had been friends for so long that there was nothing unusual about their coming and going at odd times. It was only through conversational banter that Alice had bothered to give their practised lie that Analeigh had entered a costume contest at Jackson's, left her spooky witch-book prop at home and asked for her friends to go and get it. When driving over to the house Davey had voiced concerns that the book may be hidden, but on entering her room they found that it instead lay open on her desk, proudly displayed—almost. They collected the book and headed back downstairs, but were stopped at the front door by Mrs Harris.

"My, that *is* a spooky looking book," she stated, but it was evident from her tone that this wasn't what she wanted to discuss.

"It's... very authentic," Davey agreed.

They turned to leave but before they could get far, she spoke again. "Is Analeigh... has she been acting unusual around you?"

"Yes, a bit," Davey admitted, reasoning that if her mum had noticed, then there was no point in pretending otherwise.

"You *will* look out for her, won't you?"

Davey looked to Alice but said nothing, uncertain that he could make any such promise.

"We'll do our best," answered Alice.

They drove back to Alice's and spent the night there as planned. Unlike Analeigh's decision to brazenly display the book, they chose to leave it locked in the boot of Davey's car – unwilling to have it in the house, let alone share a room with it. They did not spend the night watching movies or playing games, but instead simply lay in the dark and discussed with little optimism what tomorrow might bring. To avoid answering difficult questions, Davey's cheek had been covered with a bandage ever since Analeigh had miraculously healed it. Now, despite the wound showing no trace of having ever existed, he found himself rubbing the bandage thoughtfully and hoping that when they confronted Mother Bombalan in the morning, her raven would not be there.

Sunday, November 1st. 6:00am.

When the first rays of morning light shone in through Alice's window, the pair roused themselves quickly and readied to go. For Alice and Davey, Halloween night had been long and restless. Barely able to sleep and full of adrenaline, they had lain in darkness, awake and fearful, their minds too focused on the task ahead and the dangers they may face.

What they were about to do, Davey feared, bordered on insanity and Alice could hardly disagree. Even disregarding the threat of magic, returning to a place that you had burglarised for the express purpose of confronting the owner was reckless. However, such magical elements could not simply be disregarded. Mother Bombalan was clearly spiteful and vengeful – what was happening to Analeigh was enough to make that evident – and it was now obvious that her powers were *very* real. Despite these dangers, as they entered the car and began the trip, Davey could still imagine no alternative.

They drove out of town and up Hansen Road and, as the vehicle wound its way past the broken curve with wilted flowers, he shuddered at the reminder of why they must do what they were doing. They must confront the witch Bombalan because, even if it did end in failure – or worse – the situation that Analeigh found herself in came from a place of kindness. She – *they* – had only stolen the book because Analeigh felt that it was wrong to abandon a friend in need. She had been the best of them. The one who was unable to rest knowing that Ryan was suffering. She was the one who had pushed for them to step up and do the right thing. And now the friend in need was Analeigh and so – whatever the outcome – confront Mother Bombalan they must.

Pulling the car to a stop in the exact student parking space they had used on the night they stole the book, the pair each took a heavy breath, then exited the vehicle. Wordlessly they walked past the oval on which two teams were setting up and into the forest. Even now, during the early morning, with bright Sun shining, it took less than a few metres into the thick canopy of leaves before the atmosphere grew dark and cold. Unlike the last two times they had walked through the forest towards the old hut, neither Davey nor Alice bothered to wonder whether or not Mother Bombalan's magic was real.

They knew.

As they walked the unmarked path, Davey found his mind returning to where it had dwelled the night prior. He had lain awake in Alice's room attempting to consider all possible outcomes from the encounter they were about to initiate. His thoughts had run through the various fairy tales and mythologies that he had studied while searching for a new worldview. Collectively they had warned of a variety of dangers to be expected when crossing a witch. These dangers ranged from the largely benign (warts or rashes) to the absurd and comical (being turned into frogs or fattened up on candy and eaten). A month ago he would have considered such possibilities laughable, but since then he had seen a ghost, witnessed his friend perform miracles and horrors, and had been set upon by a large, angry bird. Now he accepted that he no longer knew what was and was not impossible and felt that any of the unlikely magical punishments he'd read of were not only conceivable but deeply terrifying. At the very least, after what Mother Bombalan had done to Analeigh, they knew for a fact she had the power to turn otherwise kind and friendly people into violent brutes. Pessimistically, he was aware that in all the conclusions to their planned meeting he had imagined, not once had he been able to envision the witch simply accepting their apology, seeing the error of her ways, and lifting Analeigh's curse.

But what else could they do?

Davey's mind tried to answer this question. He tried to form some alternative to their current plan even as they walked, but with each step taken his mind drew blanks. Soon they were in the clearing where Mother Bombalan's hut stood, and any chance to do otherwise had run its ground. The door to the hut was open.

Hesitantly the pair climbed the three steps, considered announcing themselves, then, thinking better of it, simply walked straight in. With the door already open, there was no bell to herald their entrance and the two friends went directly to the counter and waited.

An awkward minute passed between them, as they locked eyes and dared one another to call out.

"It was your idea," whispered Alice.

"You've got the book," countered Davey.

"Exactly. *I* carried the book."

"Fine," he conceded. He drew in a heavy breath, then started to shout, "Mo—" but before even the first syllable had escaped his mouth, the bead curtain parted and Mother Bombalan stepped through.

"Sorry to keep you waiting," she began in her thick European accent and then, seeing who it was, dropped it and flatly said, "Oh, it's you."

"Yes," said Davey nervously, feeling no victory in having correctly guessed that her accent was just for the tourists.

"Where is the other one? There were three of you last time," said Bombalan.

Davey glanced at Alice and she flushed red. "We came to return your book and apologise for taking it and to ask you to please forgive us and un-hex Analeigh and please don't be mad because we only wanted to help a friend and we don't even *have* two thousand dollars and your other request was completely unreasonable," she rambled in one fast and unbroken sentence, holding up the stolen book as if it were a tray of cookies.

The witch blinked once, twice, and then three times. Taking the book, she shook her head to clear it. "Could you run that by me again?"

181

This time Davey took the initiative. "We stole your book to help a friend. We thought we were doing the right thing, but acknowledge now that we acted wrongly. We are now returning the book, apologising, and ask that you please remove the hex or curse you placed on Analeigh – our third friend," he explained with patient slowness, as Alice nodded along.

The witch looked between the pair and then broke out into laughter which, to their surprise, was less of a cackle than either expected. She doubled over to catch her breath and then slowly stood back up to her regular impressive height, wiping a tear from her eye. "Firstly, I don't hex people... usually," she began, "and secondly, I'm not angry you stole my book."

"But the raven!" Alice objected.

"Sebastian is basically a guard dog and you broke into my hut! I'm not thrilled you robbed me – don't get me wrong – but I'm not mad. Certainly not *curse someone* mad. Besides, I understand more than most people that sometimes you've got to do what you've got to do. Mainly I was just impressed that you kids had the tenacity and conviction to harvest a soul!"

This time it was Alice's and Davey's turn to be confused, they shared an uncertain glance.

"Why would you assume we harvested a soul?" Alice asked slowly. "All we wanted the book for was to fix a ghost..." she trailed off.

"Right, you wanted to fix a ghost, *spirits tattered like garments*, I believe was the metaphor I gave you," said Bombalan, nodding.

"We didn't harvest any souls," Davey interjected.

"Then you didn't follow the book."

"*Tattered like garments...*" Alice repeated and then trailed off again, a worried look forming across her face.

Davey caught her concern, but had not yet reached her conclusion. "What?" he simply asked, neither directly to Alice nor to the witch.

"You need thread to repair garments," answered Alice. "What kind of thread is used to repair a spirit?"

Davey's eyes widened. He had wondered what kind of energy Analeigh was using to perform her magic and what kind of physical matter Ryan's spirit had been made of, but he had not considered that the energy Analeigh was wielding and the spirit itself were one and the same. "You mean that damage to a soul can only be repaired – *patched* – with parts taken from another soul?" he asked Alice, then, spinning on the witch, demanded, "What would happen if the ritual was performed without a harvested soul?"

Mother Bombalan looked infuriatingly indifferent. "Then whoever performed the ritual without having a soul to draw upon would draw upon their own. It's *soul weaving*. Soul. Magic. Magic that utilises the energy of a soul to be performed. It's all in the book," she said.

"Analeigh couldn't read the book. It's barely coherent... she just followed the diagrams!" Alice said breathlessly, panic rising in her throat.

"It is a complicated text," answered Bombalan, nodding sympathetically. "That's why I would have charged two thousand to study it."

"Two grand and a soul," whispered Alice.

"Yes, payment and ingredients," nodded the witch.

"That wasn't clear!" moaned Alice, temper and panic fighting for supremacy.

"You didn't ask for clarification," Bombalan coolly responded.

"You *knew* this would happen, didn't you?"

"It was your choice to steal the book," the witch shrugged.

Alice drew in a shaky breath and tried to centre herself. This argument was pointless. All that mattered now was Analeigh and what could be done to help her. "Mother Bombalan," she said with deference, "our friend *has* been using the book, not just to repair Ryan's spirit, but also to perform a great many other spells. She never harvested a soul and so, if what you are saying is true, then she has been drawing energy from her own. She is not acting like herself... we thought you had cursed her for what we did... but if you didn't and what you are saying is true, then what can we do to help her?"

The witch laughed again, but this time it *was* distinctly sinister. "If she gave her soul in bits and pieces to that dead boy by the road and has since then further torn away other parts so recklessly, then I dare say she hasn't much soul left!"

"A soul can run out?" asked Alice softly.

"All energy is finite." answered the witch.

"Conservation of matter," Davey muttered, taking no joy in learning that, as his theories were proven true, Analeigh's prospects worsened.

"And if she runs out?" pressed Alice.

"Then she becomes worse than dead. To wield soul magic is to experience a power that is addictive and – if drawn from your own soul – deeply corrupting. Our souls are what give us positive emotional feelings. It is these feelings that give morality weight and goodness purpose. She has tasted the power of soul magic and it is not a power that one gives up easily. Without a soul of her own, she will have no scruples about where she replenishes this energy from. Your friend is becoming a wraith witch, if she's not one already. A vampire of the soul. She will harm people and she will kill people, because only that will maintain her power."

"Analeigh would *never* do that! She would never – " Alice paused, catching herself in a lie.

"Never harm anyone?" the witch finished with a smile. "It has already begun then. Be wary of her. You both have what she wants. Your friend will harvest a soul. Be careful it is not your own."

Alice turned to Davey, pleading in silence for him to find a way.

"What... what can we do?" he asked hoarsely.

Mother Bombalan strode out from behind the dusty counter and began to collect trinkets from the shelves and cabinets around the room. Having gotten what she needed, she returned. "This is angel's bane – it costs four hundred dollars, and this is a soul anchor – fifty dollars," she said, placing an egg and a small gold-framed pendant holding a white gem onto the counter. Then, reaching into her own robe, she withdrew a large jagged blade. "And this is a knife," she added, placing it beside the egg and pendant.

"We want to help her, not hurt her," Davey stressed, pushing the knife away from the other two items.

"Take the dagger. It's free anyway – a wraith witch in town isn't good for anyone. The rest will cost you four fifty."

Davey fished out $15 from his wallet and promised he would pay the rest later. The witch hesitated, then agreed, while Alice collected the egg and inspected it closely.

"Angel's bane," she repeated uncertainly, rolling the egg around in her hand and trying to avoid looking at the horrible blade that still sat on the counter.

"Fake souls. Break it and pour its contents out in a field or a clearing under the moonlight. It works as bait: any creature hungry for souls will be drawn to it when broken and, once within its circle, will be held for a good long time. In this town, that should only be your little wraith," explained the witch.

"And the pendant?" asked Alice.

"A soul anchor. She's torn her spirit to shreds and so, like the boy on Hansen Road, will be stuck in limbo. Whatever is left of her fractured soul can be tied to the pendant. Soak it in her blood and then bury it with her. That way, you won't have any more nuisance ghosts hanging around town... or looking for revenge."

Davey and Alice shot a glance at each other.

"*Bury it with her*?" echoed Alice.

"We told you, we want to help her, not hurt her," repeated Davey with growing anger.

"So talk to her. The angel's bane will give you plenty of time to try, and fail. And then, when you have failed, you've got the knife and you've got the pendant. But while you're showing undue sympathy towards the wraith, beware, because if she's been doing as much as you say she has, then she's probably running low on her own energy and is not long from killing another."

"She hasn't killed anyone. She *won't*," Alice shot back.

"And we are *not* killing her," added Davey.

"Then she'll kill, and kill again," shrugged Bombalan.

Alice and Davey shared another look, this time of terror.

"Take the knife," said the witch, placing it into Alice's hand. "And don't just hurt her. You make sure she's dead."

Sunday, November 1st. 7:30am.

The walk back from the witch's hut was silent. Neither Alice nor Davey knew what to say and so said nothing, and it wasn't until they were back in Davey's car – winding their way down Hansen Road – before one of them spoke again.

"Do you believe what she said?" asked Alice, staring at her handbag and the dagger it contained.

Davey thought over his response. He hadn't really considered the possibility that Bombalan was lying. Everything the witch said had made too much sense.

So far as any of this did.

"I don't want to believe it, but I think we should keep a close eye on her," he finally answered.

"In case we need to kill her," replied Alice flatly.

"To make sure she doesn't harm anyone, or herself," he countered.

"I can't kill her." whispered Alice and silence resumed for the remainder of the drive.

Sunday, November 1st. 9:30am.

Davey's shift at the hardware store had started half an hour ago. He hadn't gone. He hadn't seen the point. Selling people tools and garden gadgets only hours after learning that your friend had possibly become an inhuman monster simply did not appeal to him. Instead, he had returned with Alice to her home and called his father from the kitchen, informing him that he wouldn't be coming in. There had been a few accusatory words directed his way – such as 'lazy' and 'spoilt' – but Davey had barely heard them and had replaced the phone back onto the cradle while the verbal tirade was still pouring out. If it was truly only a matter of time before Analeigh felt the need to kill, then this was a problem that had to be dealt with immediately, not after work.

Sitting down at the small circular table in Alice's kitchen and grateful that neither her sister nor father were home, they had started to discuss and plan what could be done. Alice wasn't fully sure she trusted Mother Bombalan – that much she made immediately clear. It was, after all, Mother Bombalan who had exposed them to the book and its dark magic, and it was only Mother Bombalan who appeared capable of reading the book's indecipherable text. Choosing to do research of their own, they pored over their many books on magic, curses and corruption, hoping to either disprove or verify Analeigh's loss of soul for themselves. As the next several hours unfolded, much to their growing distress, their research began to make the truth of Bombalan's claims increasingly apparent. It was verified again and again that the symptoms Analeigh was exhibiting – rage, violence, and extreme fatigue – were more often associated with that of corruption, and not curse. Despite this, Alice remained steadfast in her conviction that, regardless of how bad Analeigh had become and how far the corruption had reached, her friend would under no circumstances take the life of another living being. Davey was less certain but kept these thoughts to himself, reasoning that arguing over how far gone Analeigh's moral compass was did not bring them any closer to confronting her.

Pouring coffee and making toast for the two of them, Alice began to rehearse what possible conversation she could have to sway her friend. "You've been acting kind of... off, lately," she tried, speaking to Davey as her Analeigh-surrogate.

"Probably not direct enough," he criticised. How about, "The witch warned us you might have no soul and could be dangerous."

"Not funny and probably *too* direct," said Alice, stricken, but Davey wasn't trying to be funny. She finished her coffee and absentmindedly paced the room, stopping only when her attention was caught by flashing lights coming from the living room. Entering the room, she saw that the TV had been left on with the sound set to zero, and that the news was mutely running a special broadcast.

The reporter stood in front of a forest and behind her several police officers were keeping busy. As a feeling of dread formed in her throat, Alice strained her eyes, but was unable to make out the words of the news ticker that scrolled its small ribbon of information across the bottom of the screen.

"Alice?" asked Davey from the kitchen.

Vaguely she noted that the clump of forest where the reporter stood resembled the treeline not far beyond Jackson's property. Coming out of the trees, two people in white lab coats walked behind the reporter carrying a stretcher with a white cloth that hung over a horrible shape. "There's something on the TV..." muttered Alice, so quietly that Davey barely heard.

The writing continued to scroll across the bottom of the screen, while the reporter continued her muted dialogue. Reluctantly Alice took a step closer towards the television in order to get a better view of the news ticker's writing, but it was mid-loop, the start having already scrolled away.

"What?" asked Davey.

The text looped past for a second run. "Body of teenage boy found. Foul play suspected." it declared, and Alice let out a strangled sob.

Sunday, November 1st. 6:00pm.

"The body of a young male has been found in the woods just outside the Clarke Valley town limits. The deceased has not yet been identified, but police suspect foul play was involved and are now looking through missing persons reports. The body – discovered mostly naked – was found wearing costume inflatable gloves, although police say that the level of decomposition would suggest the crime took place long before last night's Halloween festivities."

The report had been running all day, repeated on every local news station, each parroting the same words and using identical b-roll footage. None of the reports mentioned that it was Cole. They were likely not yet even aware he was missing. But Alice knew. Alice had known the moment she saw the bulletin, recognised the treeline, and heard about the inflatable gloves. Had she and Davey stayed the night at Jackson's, they would have witnessed Analeigh leaving early with Cole. Had they stayed at Jackson's until dinnertime the next evening, they would have seen the frenzied visit from Cole's mother, who – sparked by the news reports – was worried that her son had yet returned home.

They knew that they couldn't allow their friend to continue the cycle of violence Mother Bombalan suggested had now begun, but what could they do to stop her? Briefly they debated calling the police but decided against it, reasoning that two 17-year-olds wouldn't get very far trying to convince the authorities their victim had been murdered by a teenage witch.

Oh, by the way, officer, she also likely stole his soul.

Even if they were able to convince the police, they couldn't help but wonder what might come of Analeigh's arrest. Would she face jail for murder and remain forever corrupted? Would she suffer endlessly from fits of rage and anger? Or would she be helped? *Could she be helped?* They doubted that the law would believe, let alone attempt to remedy, the damage Analeigh had caused herself.

Unless Analeigh doesn't give them the chance to not believe, Davey thought glumly.

There was, he reflected, nothing stopping Analeigh from proving beyond any doubt that her abilities were real. She could do it, perhaps in a fit of rage and delirium, or while attempting to escape, or merely out of boredom. If she were to do this, then the fears that Analeigh herself had earlier voiced would surely come true. She would no doubt be subjected to horrible government experimentation. She would face dissection at the hands of nameless agents in black from secret government wings – the MKUltras, and the Project Blue Books or whatever unofficial forces carry out government secrets in the shadows. When Davey put these concerns to Alice, they caused her to shudder, but even that was not the worst-case scenario.

Reluctantly, Davey had pointed out that there was no real reason to believe Analeigh, if caught, would go quietly. She had puppeteered Cole around as easily as she had Claire's doll and there was nothing preventing her from doing the very same to any law enforcement unlucky enough to be sent her way. For a split second Davey's imagination had horribly flared and he had experienced a vision of police officers surrounding Analeigh's house and her coming out twitching and writhing while the police drew their guns and fired on one another. He hadn't explained this exact scenario to Alice, but she had an imagination of her own.

Fearing this possibility of collateral damage, Alice and Davey eventually agreed that if anyone were to confront Analeigh, it must be them. In deciding this, they chose to talk to Analeigh without any deception and without the use of the angel's bane. They felt that to imprison her within the witch Bombalan's trap would likely make the chance of open dialogue more difficult, and they hoped that by talking to her in a friendly setting and explaining their fears of what she might continue to do to herself and others, then surely they would be able to appeal to her better judgement. They felt that if they could get her to see what she had become, then they could convince her to go with them to Bombalan and together press, plead, and perhaps even force the forest witch to find a solution and restore Analeigh to her old self.

Alice was not willing to accept that this was not a possibility.

Settling on this approach of friendly intervention, the pair began attempts to meet with Analeigh on her own terms. They called the Harris residence hoping to speak to her, but no one came to the phone and the call rang out. It was already getting dark and the fact that neither Analeigh nor her parents were home caused Alice and Davey to immediately grow concerned. Taking Davey's car, they sped towards Analeigh's house, where on arrival they found the driveway empty and the windows of the house smashed outwards. The glass combined with the scattered and shattered plastic skeletons and foam tombstones of Analeigh's obliterated Halloween decorations made the front yard look as though someone had set off a bomb in a cemetery. The livingroom curtains were tattered and blew in the wind like the damaged sails of a destroyed ship and briefly Davey wondered what their English teacher, Mr Bowden, might have said about their symbolism.

The door was unlocked – most doors in Clarke Valley were – and the inside of Mrs Harris's usually neat home looked as though it had been ransacked. Furniture was strewn about, wallpaper shredded. Shelves from cabinets, books, and photos littered the floor. They searched from room to room and quickly realised that the house was deserted. Breaking off from Davey, Alice climbed the stairs to Analeigh's bedroom, only to find that it too had been left in a similar state of disarray. Idly she wondered if Analeigh had done this while in a fury after discovering that the book was missing or if her actions had come from an unrelated fit of rage. They wondered about the fate of her parents and hoped that their cars not being in the driveway indicated they had not been home when this had happened. The two friends then considered whether or not they themselves were in any immediate danger for having taken the book or if Analeigh knew that it had already been returned to Bombalan.

Whatever the case, after seeing what Analeigh had done to her own home, the pair now accepted that there would be no sitting her down in a place of mutual meeting for calm and rational discussion. If there was any chance that she was going to listen to what they had to say, then she would have to be made to.

Returning to Alice's home once more, they collected the egg and then, after a heated debate, also took the pendant and the knife.

The Sun had long since set and the Moon had risen.

In sorrow and in fear, they drove with the three items in their possession to the school's oval, which looked down upon the town from atop the dark twists and blind turns of Hansen Road.

Sunday, November 1st. 11:30pm.

It was late evening by the time Davey pulled his car to a stop in the deserted student parking lot of Clarke Valley High. No sports matches and no team practice take place this late on a Sunday and beyond themselves, not a soul was in sight. The oval that sat before them was basked in blue moonlight and damp with evening dew.

They had argued, they had yelled, and they had cried.

After seeing her house, it had been decided that they would use the angel's bane to bait and hold Analeigh – but only to talk. They would confront her about the body, convince her that she needed help, and keep her there until she saw the truth in what they said. Despite the passive and nonviolent nature of their plan, Alice had reluctantly agreed to bring along the knife and pendant – for their own protection, if for nothing else.

Seeing how strongly she felt about the dagger, Davey had offered to carry the blade himself, but Alice had refused. She had insisted that if it were kept concealed within her handbag it would be less conspicuous to anyone who might see them and less likely to cause Analeigh anger. In truth, she had made this insistence for the express purpose of keeping it on her person and not Davey's. She wanted to have full control over its use. It was, she thought, only through her carrying the dagger that she could be certain it would not be used. No matter how much Analeigh raved and ranted, and no matter how aggressive she seemed, Alice planned for the blade to never leave her handbag. Despite this self-assurance of intention to never take the knife out, she had checked that it still sat within her small black bag several times during the short drive towards the school.

Davey carried the egg and pendant, and Alice carried the knife.

Reaching the centre of the oval, Alice opened her mouth, closed it – thought – and then opened it again. "I don't believe she will try to hurt us," she said, more to herself than to Davey.

It was a discussion that they'd had a dozen times since returning the book to Mother Bombalan and a dozen more since the news had reported a body found. Davey now feared that this could possibly be the last time they would be able to have it. He rolled the egg over in his hand and felt unable to meet Alice's eyes. "And if she does?" he asked gravely.

Alice gave no response and he let out a rattled sigh.

They had both seen what Analeigh had done to Cole in the classroom, how cruel she had been at the party, and the destruction at her house... and then there was the dead body. Davey thought about how grey her skin had become and how dull her eyes had dimmed. He thought about the ominous warning Mother Bombalan had given and the endless chapters on corruption they had read in their various books on magic. He hoped that Bombalan's angel's bane would hold Analeigh long enough for them to talk, but he had no doubt that their imminent interaction would be hostile – violent, even.

Wanting to make sure Alice was prepared for what they were about to face, he chose his words carefully. "We saw her house, Alice. She *is* dangerous and we shouldn't expect she won't be towards us."

"She's our best friend," Alice shot back. "We owe her a chance to beat this."

This time Davey did meet her eyes and saw tears within them. "I just hope she gives us a chance," he answered flatly.

He held up the small egg and examined it in the moonlight. Aside from it being as white as paper, it looked no different from any ordinary chicken egg and briefly his cynical-self re-emerge to dully hope that the witch hadn't sold them snake oil.

"Bombalan says the egg will both draw her in and hold her. She'll *have* to listen. We'll make her," Alice promised.

Davey hoped that she was right. "Are you ready?" he asked.

Alice nodded, subconsciously touching her hand to her bag, and Davey broke the egg.

The contents of the egg was thick and oozing. From the shell, it sludged more than it poured and, as the light of the Moon drifted behind a sea of clouds, it became obvious that that which had been contained glowed radiant. Reaching the grass, the luminous white slime puddled and spread beyond that which the size of the egg would have suggested possible. Warily, Davey and Alice stepped backwards to avoid the expanding glow, which soon reached its zenith as a perfectly even circle of about 5 metres in diameter.

"Did it work?" blinked Alice.

"Something happened." answered Davey, uncertain as to what it was a magical egg should do. "If that witch Bombalan..." he began and then fell silent as the whole world seemed to flicker before his eyes.

The security lights over at the school, the streetlights on the road, the house lights down in Clarke Valley, and the very stars themselves seemed to blink out. Beyond the school, even the unnoticed but ever-present hum of the nearby power station ceased. All was pitch black except for the disk of white angel's bane that glowed as a midnight sun. Soon even that blinked, then slowly light returned and dead centre within the glowing circle stood their friend Analeigh.

Her skin was asphalt, her eyes smoke with red pupils. She knelt and ran her hand through the white goop – her

fingers seeming as though they lengthened to meet it –
and she hissed at what they found.

"Ani, we need to talk," said Alice faintly.

Analeigh stood slowly and walked towards her friends,
who took equal and involuntary steps backwards. Having
reached the circumference of the circle, she jerked to a
stop – as though she were a dog caught by its leash. "What
is this?" she demanded.

"Angel's bane," answered Davey.

A flush of pink returned to Analeigh's flesh and a
glimpse of humanity showed. "I can't leave. Why can't
I leave?" she asked, suddenly sounding small and very
frightened.

Alice drew closer to her friend, reclaiming one of her
retreated steps. "You can't leave because we were worried
you would try to," she said softly. "We need to talk to you
and you need to listen."

"How *dare* you keep me here, what gives you the
right?!" Analeigh screamed into Alice's face and what
little colour had shown quickly vanished.

"This is why!" responded Davey, his anger at how
Analeigh had acted towards them and others over the last
week now boiling to the surface. "You've been acting like
a total lunatic!"

At this, Analeigh broke down and began to cry. "You're
right," she wept. "It's all this magic and I can't help it. It's
like there is a small me – a child – watching what I've

become from far away, but the child is also me and I hate her with all my heart," she moaned and fell to her knees.

Alice took another step forward, while Davey followed hesitantly. In the brightness of the angel's bane Analeigh was nothing more than a small silhouette that appeared to shrink before their eyes.

"Oh Ani," said Alice.

She moved to take another step closer, but her advance was halted by Davey, who held out his arm across her chest.

"You hurt Cole, didn't you?" he asked softly, already feeling certain that both he and Alice knew the answer.

"The teeth," she moaned. "It was horrible of me."

Davey was unsatisfied. "Did you *kill* Cole?" he demanded. "Was he the body we saw on the news?"

The sobbing stopped and the dark figure seemed to return to its previous size. Then, immediately and without having moved, she was pressed against the invisible barrier of the angel's bane – as close to Davey as the circle would allow. "He was wasted energy. Think of the good I can do with what he gave me," she spat.

"With what you took," Davey corrected.

"So it *is* true," whispered Alice. She had already known the truth in her heart, but hearing it confirmed mortified her all the same.

"He was a monster, Alice. He killed Ryan," answered Analeigh.

"Don't pretend you did this for Ryan, you have no right—" began Davey.

"—I have every right," Analeigh coldly cut in.

"Please, Ani, we can get you help – I'm sure... just stop this, please. We know it isn't you... we know it's the magic that's done this. Come with us, we'll take you to see Mother Bombalan and we'll find a way to fix this," Alice begged.

Analeigh laughed. "Don't you see? This – this is a *good* thing, Alice. There won't be any more cruelty, any more blowhards or bullies. Don't you understand? I can take their energy and use it to stop them! With what Cole gave me, I could stop five Coles, and from them twenty-five! I could end wars, topple dictatorships! Can't you see what I could do for this world with the powers I've been given?"

"You've not been *given* anything, Ani," answered Davey. "You've taken it. And what you did to Cole was worse than anything he *ever* did to Ryan, or me. We can't let you do this. Our friend – the person you used to be – would not have wanted it."

Analeigh smiled, and started to pace back and forth like a lion eyeing its prey. "You can't stop me. This won't hold me."

"Mother Bombalan seems to think it will."

"That hag Bombalan was a weak fool, she hoarded my book but refused to learn from it. I won't make the same mistake," she promised and started to contort and twist her arms and fingers.

"There's noth—" Davey started, then screamed and fell to his knees as ribbons of energy began to twist and snake their way from his pores, his eyes, and his very being.

"Please, stop," Alice sobbed.

"You force this, Alice. You could have freed me. You could have been my friend. But now I'll have to free myself." The wraith witch ranted while Davey shook violently, his torn soul continuing to flow towards her, as she danced her demonic dance.

"Analeigh," whispered Alice.

"You betrayed me, Alice. You and your pathetic boyfriend."

"Please, Analeigh," she said, shakily reaching her hand into her bag. Vaguely, in the back of her mind, she noted with certainty that Bombalan was dead and that Davey was dying.

"He will die," Analeigh stated as though she had heard her thoughts and agreed, while Davey's energy reached the edge of the circle.

"I'm sorry," Alice whispered. She held her breath and took two steps over the precipice of the angel's bane. She walked with Mother Bombalan's blade in hand, while Analeigh continued to spasm and jangle her strange dance, too concentrated on Davey to notice her approach. They were centimetres apart and Alice could feel cold air radiating from her former friend as though she were a fridge-door left open to a summer's day.

Picking her mark, Alice closed her eyes, prayed for forgiveness, and sank the blade deep into Analeigh's back. She felt the squish of flesh and the crunch of bone as it slid through her thinned, grey skin and Analeigh let out a horrific inhuman scream that echoed across the plateau, shook the leaves in the forest, and could just-in-so be heard in the town below. Alice retrieved the blade, then drove it home once more – this time into the base of Analeigh's neck – and Davey dropped limply to the grass as Analeigh continued to scream. The blood that fell from her wounds was thick black and splattered down into the angel's bane as dark globules, while the witch thrashed about and Alice held on as though she were trying not to be thrown from some mechanical bull. From the corner of her eye, she saw that the bright streamers torn from Davey's soul were retreating away from the circle and back towards his immobile body, while Analeigh twisted her arms at impossible degrees and scratched at Alice with sharp fingernails that broke skin and drew blood. The hilt of the blade was becoming slippery with her former friend's dark ichor, but Alice held on until – with one last horrible rasp – the creature that had once been her oldest friend collapsed and Alice fell to the ground beside her.

Lying in the grass, Alice checked herself over and found that there were large chunks of skin and flesh torn from her arms and hands. Her left eye wouldn't open and she could feel thick streams of blood mixed with tears rolling down her cheek. She wanted to just sit there crying. To curl up into a ball and lie there sobbing until the Sun rose – but she knew that she didn't have that luxury. She knew that, as horrible as the task she had just performed was, the deed was not yet done. And so, pulling herself up onto her hands and knees, she scanned her surroundings with her remaining eye and looked for Davey.

His body lay sprawled awkwardly 3 metres away from her and Alice crawled towards him, wincing in pain as grass and dirt found their way into her fresh, deep wounds. Reaching him, she fumbled with his pockets, found the pendant hidden within them and crawled back. She hadn't bothered to check his pulse and she didn't stop to try and assist him – there were more pressing matters at hand than even Davey's wellbeing. Leaning over what she now refused to think of as Analeigh, Alice soaked the pendant in the corpse's thick blood – and the clear white crystal held within its small gold frame changed to a dark black. As her vision blurred and distorted, she placed the pendant around the wraith witch's neck, and fainted.

AFTERMATH

AFTERMATH

For Alice, the moments, minutes, and days that followed her plunging the knife into her former friend's neck blur and twist in her memory – distorted and surreal. She can recall the last breath of life as it had left Analeigh and how she had felt her death rattle reverberate through the blade. She can recall lying on the grass and seeing that, just as the light had faded from Analeigh's eyes, so too did the glow of the angel's bane diminish. She can recall having woken up after some unknown length of unconsciousness, bathed in the light of the Moon as a raven circled high above.

Davey would not wake up and Analeigh was dead.

Alone, Alice was forced to stumble her way to Davey's car (having fished the keys from his pocket). He had been cold to the touch, but there had been a weak pulse. He was too heavy to move and so, taking a blanket from the back of his car and wrapping him in it, Alice had left him there, intending to go for help. She had limped towards the vehicle feeling as though dark eyes were watching her, and had vaguely hoped that they belonged to Bombalan's raven and not Analeigh's fractured spirit. Collapsing into the car, she'd fumbled with the ignition and prayed to any gods who might listen that whatever was left of her former friend's energy would be held successfully by the pendant and be too weakened to cause Davey any further harm.

She could barely remember the drive back down the hill. Her left eye wouldn't open from the deep scratch it had received. Her head throbbed and her wounds burned. Her arms, neck, and face were covered in a mixture of mud, dirt, blood and Analeigh's dark ichor. A part of her had wondered whether she would go to jail for what she had done to Analeigh, but that would be a problem for another day. Instead of trying to make it home, she pulled into the first open business she saw – O'Brien's Bar. Stumbling inside and looking as though she were the living dead, she had asked the bartender to call the police and have an ambulance sent to the school, rambled something about Davey, Cole, and Analeigh, then blacked out.

She fell into a long, dreamless sleep, only to awaken the next afternoon confused, bloodied and bandaged in a Clarke Valley Hospital bed.

It was another two days until Davey regained consciousness and Alice spent that time in an endless cycle of sleeping, being questioned by Chief Braxton and avoiding calls and visits from family, friends, and reporters. As to her role in Analeigh's death, Alice claimed that what she had done had been in self-defence – which Davey would eventually echo upon awakening. Neither of them brought up magic or bothered to answer what they had been doing on the oval at night and Alice claimed that Bombalan's knife belonged to Analeigh, not to her or Davey. Though what Analeigh had done to Davey wasn't outwardly obvious, the damage to Alice was evident and

– having lost an eye in her struggle – self-defence hadn't sounded as far-fetched as she had at first worried it might.

While Alice's injuries alone were not initially enough to indicate that the fight had not been mutual, they were lent further credence by the fact that those interviewed by the police confirmed Analeigh had been acting erratically in the days leading up to her death. She had, the police quickly learned, even attacked her parents and destroyed much of the family home only hours before the altercation on the oval. Further damning was the identification of recently murdered teenager Cole Sheridan, whose final night alive was found to have been spent with Analeigh Harris.

Davey left the hospital the day he woke up, two days before Alice herself was able to. His wounds – so far as medical science was concerned – had been mostly emotional. He couldn't remember a great deal of what had happened after telling Analeigh she wouldn't be able to escape, but a visit with Alice in her hospital room filled him in. He had no recollection of his soul being torn from him, having it returned or collapsing, but felt a tremendous fatigue that would continue to plague him in the weeks and months that followed.

The first visit he made to Alice in the hospital had been difficult. He had nearly collapsed a second time when he had seen how pale and utterly destroyed she seemed, and had found it hard to meet her gaze – disturbed by the bandages that wrapped the left side of her face and the knowledge of the empty hole they covered. Her arms, chest, neck, and head were dressed in various medical strips that discoloured even during their short conversation, betraying the existence of still-weeping wounds beneath. Despite the initial awkwardness, Davey continued to visit Alice in the hospital and at her home following her release, and as they talked, they smiled, and sometimes laughed, and over time it began to seem as though, one day – despite everything – things might be normal once more.

Alice enjoyed these visits from Davey. He was the one person who truly understood. He knew what had happened that night and he shared in her lie of omission regarding Analeigh's dark magic and grizzly death. His presence reassured and grounded her. It was only when Davey was there that she felt safe from drifting into the nightmare reruns of Analeigh's sharp claws tearing at her face and the crunch of bone as she drove the dagger deep into her neck. At various points – in the middle of the night or during the middle of the day – Alice awoke in a cold sweat and struggled to remember whether or not Analeigh was dead and whether she had remembered to place the pendant around her neck. She would fight through fog and confusion as the events of the terrible evening played before her, then, recalling that she had done what had been necessary, she would lie back down and drift once more.

So long as the pendant had been soaked in her blood, Analeigh's ghost would be tied to it – unable to seek vengeance and unable to wander. The pendant had no doubt since been removed from her corpse by the coroner and was likely sitting on some metal tray in a morgue or locked up in police evidence. *That doesn't matter, though*, Alice thought. *Let her haunt the morgue for now.*

After leaving the hospital and returning home, Alice's night-terrors lessened, but would still occasionally and sporadically occur. Even years after the dark events on the oval of Clarke Valley High, she would still sometimes wake in a pool of sweat and wonder about the pendant. It wasn't until nine days after the incident that she was finally up and moving around the house – no longer spending each day entirely within her bedroom, trapped in her strange twilight dream state. She had been given a plain white-cotton eye patch by the hospital, but was now wearing the black leather one with a white Jolly Roger on it that Davey had given her from his Halloween costume.

Next year, they would both go to Jackson's party as pirates.

The missing eye itched and she found herself constantly having to resist the urge to scratch it. Depth perception was proving difficult – she had already broken two mugs while making her morning coffee. Yesterday, along with Davey, Mrs Harris had visited. She had told them through tears that she didn't blame them. She herself was sporting a broken arm that she had sustained on the night of Analeigh's death and that had been enough to convince her of just how unhinged and dangerous her daughter had become. Mrs Harris hadn't mentioned Analeigh doing anything unnatural, but there were long pauses in her account of the evening that left Alice and Davey plenty of room to guess. She had come with the purpose of checking on Alice's health and to inform her of Analeigh's pending funeral. She had asked if they intended to go and whether or not there was anything she or Davey needed. It was stressed that they were not expected to attend, especially – as Mrs Harris had put it with a sob – "all things considered". Davey had glanced at Alice and then confirmed for the both of them that they would of course be there.

After a long pause, Alice had made the simple request that Analeigh be buried with a special gold-and-black pendant she had given her as a token of their friendship.

Saturday, November 14th. 11:00am.

Just over one month ago Analeigh had never before
been to a funeral and now she was the unknown guest
of honour at her own. She sat atop her casket – invisible,
powerless, and fuming with rage – watching as the ceremony played out before her. The heavy use of soul magic
had not been kind to her body and her funeral, much like
Ryan's, was not an open-casket affair. The celebrant led a
psalm and her parents spoke, and her mother said kind
words while all those in attendance stared at the broken
arm Analeigh had given her. Aside from her close family,
and Alice and Davey who sat with empty spaces on either
side of them, the funeral chapel was sparsely populated.
With Ryan's funeral last month and Cole's only last week,
this small attendance may have been due to the residents
of Clarke Valley simply being "funeralled out," but the
more likely reason was that the town had *heard*. The
rumour mill had spun, the town had spoken and now it
was whispered that in her final days Analeigh had been a
druggy, a murderer, or worse.

*Analeigh hated them all. She hated the world, and she
hated her weakness.*

The power that she had loved so much had deserted
her. At first the use of soul magic had felt good, the way
a drunken buzz drowns out your troubles, but she had
gone too far and even the buzz had left her. Now she was
nothing but hollow, and angry. She wanted to step down
from her casket, walk into the small crowd, and kill each

and every one of them, but found herself unable to move a metre beyond her corpse and its damned pendant. Even if she did manage to break away from the soul anchor's restraint, deep down she doubted whether she would be able to exact the vengeance she so strongly desired. The weakness of her tattered spirit was pitiful – she hadn't even been able to kill Davey as he lay there that night, unconscious and alone on the sports field of Clarke Valley High. Above her Bombalan's raven had circled and cried for its former master and Analeigh had tried to leave. It was then that she had discovered that she was bound to her own corpse by the small blood-soaked pendant. If she were still wielding the power of a full soul, then Analeigh had no doubts in her mind that the pendant would have been no match for her, but she had torn and thrashed apart what little of Cole's spirit she had left when killing Bombalan and trying to escape the angel's bane, and had failed in her attempt to take from Davey a fresh soul. Now it was all that she could do to hold herself together.

Over the two weeks since her death, Analeigh had learned just how inescapable the tight leash of the small pendant was. She had been compelled to follow her corpse as it was transported from the oval to the morgue by an ambulance. The pendant was then removed and placed on a small metal tray, while her corpse was laid out on a cold bench. There Analeigh had been made to stand witness to her own autopsy as the coroner – baffled by her discoloured skin, eyes, and extended fingers – cut her open and eventually settled on no other cause of death beyond the obvious stab wounds. The pendant was then gathered up and placed into a small biohazard bag which (along with her corpse) was zipped into a body bag and transported to the town mortician. Her corpse was cleaned and embalmed, and on behalf of Alice the pendant was placed around her neck for burial – anchoring her spirit and damning Analeigh to a long eternity trapped beside her own corpse, soon to be imprisoned within a dark grave.

The small gathering was leaving now, depositing flowers onto her wooden box and retreating to the back room for weak coffee and dry biscuits. She tried in vain to follow them down the aisle and out the door, but with her best efforts was unable to move beyond the funeral lectern. Defeated, she returned to her casket, and waited. After a long half-hour, two men in dirty overalls entered the room. Bracing themselves for the weight of the casket, they lifted and began to carry out her remains. She struggled against the pull and spared one final glance towards the door at the end of the aisle beyond which her former friends and family drank, ate, and traded stories about what she had once been. A small part of Analeigh wanted to join them. To remember herself. But mostly that part of her had been traded for power and what now remained simply wanted to strip their souls and make them suffer.

The two men carried the casket out through the side door towards the waiting grave and, as the pendant moved, it tugged and pulled at her. Briefly she wondered if this was how Cole had felt while she had puppeteered him around.

Then, powerless to fight it, Analeigh followed.

CONTACT THE AUTHOR

Email:
darkwellbled@outlook.com

Twitter:
@DarkwellBled